The Pa's Eye:

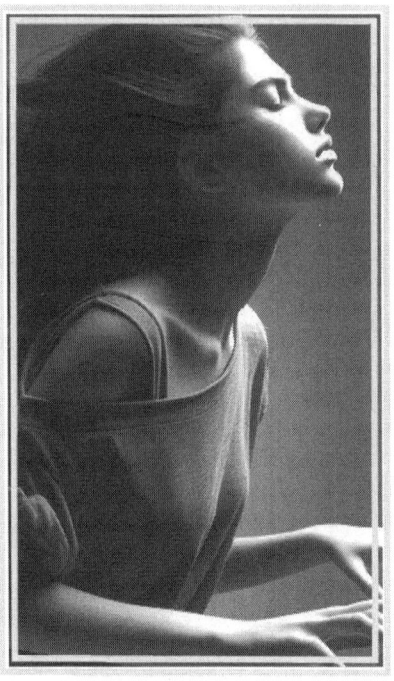

Lizzie Collins

Copyright © 2022 Lizzie Collins
All rights reserved.

Characters and events portrayed in this book are fictitious.

Any resemblance to persons living or dead is coincidental and not intended by the author

ISBN: 9798831943573

DEDICATION

To my wonderful grandchildren who are so inspirational

Isobel, James, Matilda and Lily

Thank you!

"His voice would soar to the tops of the overhanging conifers and hover there in the air, before melting into the ether. I believed, and still do, there was nothing closer to heaven on earth than hearing Gil Robson sing in these mountains."

Giulia Giordano Robson

The Story So Far

Naive seventeen-year-old Connie Meyer, protected child of a wealthy family, meets and marries Gil Robson, two years older and with a troubled past.

But Gil had been married long before – to his music.

'Catch A Falling Star', the first book in the 'Ultimate Link' series, is the story of their doomed marriage, and the shocking damage it does to the lives of their two little boys.

Overcome by crushing loneliness from Gil's tours and work commitments, Connie has an affair with Oliver Maxwell, an attractive and wealthy Los Angeles businessman.

As a result of the stress and inadequacy Gil feels from the loss of his wife, he is drawn into his brother Jamie's dark, destructive world of drink and drugs.

Jacob and Mylo, his and Connie's sons, are caught in the crossfire, and had they not been rescued by a doting grandmother - the Robsons' mother Nancy - might have been abandoned completely.

Gil attempts to get his life back on track with the help of Giulia Giordano, spoilt daughter of a major Hollywood entertainer. The whole Giordano family befriended Gil from childhood and Paul and Carrie Giordano became surrogate parents through his most troubled years. At first her advances puzzle him as he still thinks of Giulia as a little sister.

Then Gil's adored brother dies in an accident on his yacht, and Connie briefly gets drawn into his life again.

While accidentally meeting at Jamie's grave, their emotions give way to one final act of love, which leads to a disastrous pregnancy, shocking to them both.

Fearing a repeat of the damage to their two sons, Connie hides their little girl from Gil, determined she should have a full and happy childhood. Gil is devastated.

Giulia attempts to lift him from his debilitating depression by gifting him what she perceives to be his heart's desire.

Meanwhile, Gil and Connie's baby daughter is growing up safe, happy and in total ignorance half a continent away in Illinois.

This is her story.

Prologue by Christie

I didn't find out about some of these happenings until many of the people involved were well on in years and much of the tensions in their lives had, thankfully, faded. Some have temporarily left us along the way.

Gil and Connie's divorce was finalized a couple of years after my birth, which sent the goddamn fool into another spiral of self-indulgence, meaning he totally fucked up the record deal Harry and David had so painstakingly set up. It was a while until they spoke to him again. I'd have shot him dead.

No record label would deal with the three of them once Gil started sticking white stuff up his nose again and renewed his friendship with Jack Daniels. I asked him later what kind of bastard does that to his best friends, and he shrugged, but I could read him like a book by this time, so was aware of his deep shame. I think Harry and David started talking to him again from terror, afraid he might dump his problems on them all over again.

Meanwhile, in an attempt to straighten himself out, he had married Giulia somewhere obscure. As far as I'm aware no-one else went to the ceremony other than Giulia's mother and her brothers – even Jacob and Mylo didn't bother, and who could blame them. He did once tell me where it was, but I can't remember.

What I do remember though was that Carrie Giordano, Giulia's mother, was fit to be tied and didn't speak to Pa again from that day forward – which was a total waste of her time because I doubt he even noticed.

Towards the end of my story, I have let everyone involved have their say. Not one of us could see eye to eye with any other which makes for an uneasy life but a good story. Anyway, now back to the task in hand.

PART ONE

Chapter One

Who is Christie Heywood?

My name is Anna Christina Heywood but everyone calls me Christie. I was thirteen last birthday.

I live in Champaign, Illinois, with my mother Catherine and my father Julius, who works at the University. I don't know exactly what he does, but I do know he's important. My mother's told me so on a number of occasions – usually when I've misbehaved and I might cause him embarrassment.

I have long, straight ink-black hair which my mother plaits. Often, I go down to the Arboretum where hidden amongst the trees, I unplait it and let it free. For some reason I don't understand, Mom doesn't seem to like it like that, so I go home through the kitchen door, so she doesn't see.

My eyes are dark brown which is puzzling as my father's eyes are grey-green and my mother's bright blue. She has hair so fair it catches the sun.

My father doesn't smile much - I don't know why. Sometimes, he brings me paints and pencils. I love to sketch, especially the tree blossoms in Spring, but I'm not too good with color yet.

I've lots of good school friends, but my very best buddy is Jenny who lives near my Auntie Grace in Windham, Illinois. Sometimes, if Mom and Dad have to be away, I am allowed to stay for a few days, and

Jenny and I talk about boys and popstars in my room. We collect pictures and put them in private albums with little locks on them.

Under my bed I hide the child-sized guitar my auntie bought me for my eighth birthday. It was our little secret said Auntie Grace, so not even Jenny knows about it. Grace said she'd arrange lessons for me when I was older if I was interested.

To tell the truth, I'm not particularly. I like playing the piano in the drawing-room though. I seem to be able to hear a tune a couple of times and find the right keys pretty quickly. Now I am thirteen, I can play with both hands which is much harder but much more fun. I might ask auntie if I can have piano lessons for my birthday.

Auntie Grace is my favorite person in the whole world. She does crazy things like pretend to hate pizza, then the hugest pizza ever is delivered for Jenny and me to scarf down in the garden treehouse. She sends us there, she says, so she doesn't have to watch us eat like pigs. She always gives a little secret smile when she says it though.

Auntie Grace has a son she doesn't like. I'm to call him Oliver, but for some reason I don't understand, I've to call his girlfriend Auntie Connie. She cries a lot.

One day when I was at Windham and Oliver had gone back to Los Angeles where he lives, I overheard a conversation in the conservatory which puzzled me.

"When will we be able to tell her?" asked Auntie

Connie.

"You know that just can't happen, Connie. Not for the foreseeable future anyway. He would be sure to find her if you got any closer than here. Here, your visits aren't suspicious as I'm Oliver's mother, but if you start taking trips around rural Illinois, it's going to be a different story. More tea?"

"No thanks." There was a clatter of china, as Connie replaced her cup and saucer on the little walnut table.

"Come on, dear. Let's take a walk in the garden. I'll drive you to O'Hare first thing. You'll make the morning plane in plenty of time. I'll call Oliver to pick you up in LA."

They stood to leave, so I tiptoed as quickly as I could to hide behind the staircase.

As they walked through the door, arm in arm, Auntie Grace turned round, looked at the stairs and said in a loud voice:

"You can come out now."

Then they were gone. I forgot to say that I thought Auntie Grace had psychic powers.

Dad came to collect me the following afternoon. He took tea with Auntie Grace, looking as uncomfortable as he always did. I never could figure out why. Auntie Grace clearly liked him since she offered him tea in the first place. She didn't do that for everyone. I determined to ask him why in the car on the way home.

"Dad, why don't you like Auntie Grace?"

"Who says I don't?" he replied.

"Well, you never even take off your jacket, or laugh at her jokes, or anything."

"What jokes? In all the time I've known her, I've never heard Grace say anything even remotely funny."

I looked at him closely. Was he joking? Auntie Grace had the best sense of humor of anyone I knew. But his eyes were fixed on the road ahead, and he looked lost in thought.

There was a long, long uncomfortable silence before I tackled my next question.

"Dad. Why don't I look like you and Mom? I look odd. Even Jenny's noticed. Auntie Grace always changes the subject when I ask and takes me to buy a sweater or to the movies."

That got his attention. I felt rather than saw him jump, but he stayed with his eyes fixed on the road and didn't reply. This mystery was making me crazy. I found myself thinking about it whenever my mind wasn't fixed on something else. Auntie Grace was still my best bet. Mom would just take Dad's side.

But it was like hitting a brick wall. Finally, Auntie Grace told me, if I didn't hold my tongue, I couldn't come again.

Auntie Connie didn't visit as often after that, and when she did, she cried more than usual, which was saying something.

Over time, I put it to the back of my mind.

Chapter Two

Of Pianos and Pixies

It was a couple of years before anything else of note happened.

I learned that Dad was Head of the Faculty of Mathematics. I would make excuses to visit him there from time to time; packed lunch he'd forgotten – he always ate in the University dining hall – or a book I'd stolen from his briefcase, so I could return it.

His study smelled of bees-wax and old books. There was a pink blotter on a heavy old-fashioned desk, and floor to ceiling shelves full of books with titles like 'Mathematics and Probability' and 'The Mathematics of Quantum Physics'. Mind-blowingly boring.

If I examined what I was good at, it certainly wasn't anything like mathematics, which meant most sciences were out of my reach. What was I good at? Damned if I knew.

Auntie Grace had come up with the goods on the music lessons. We tried the guitar first. She bought me a full-sized one and told me it would be so cool to be another Bob Dylan or Joni Mitchell. I only had a vague recollection of who they were, as my favorite crush of the time were the Bee Gees. Finally, even she gave up on me.

So then we moved to the piano, which I'd loved from the moment I first ran my fingers over the keys.

I didn't know why she insisted I was a guitarist, but Auntie Grace was a determined woman.

With the piano I began down the traditional road of classical lessons, but I was bored to tears by Beethoven and Rachmaninov.

Eventually, thanks to Elton John and his boogie-woogie, I found something I was really good at. My piano teacher was horrified when I turned 'Fur Elisa' into something Jerry Lee might have been proud of. I may not know Bob Dylan but I knew all the rock n roll piano players. On one of the very rare occasions I saw Auntie Grace laugh out loud, she'd noticed the expression on the music teacher's face. Then she sacked him and told me I'd to practice an hour morning and afternoon every day.

She also told my Dad to buy a piano, which he did. I think he'd the Beethoven thing more in mind, until I started practicing. Then he went back to work more often, and my mother had sudden engagements at a friend's house. I didn't care. I was having a whale of a time. Auntie Grace's two hours a day turned into as many as I could manage.

The other thing I was good at was painting. I'd progressed from the blossom pencil sketches to a more impressionistic painting style. I'd always liked pastel colors like Monet used but, recently I'd started doing my own thing, and had begun using different, more vibrant shades. I still liked trees though and spent any hours not at school or the piano, at the Arboretum.

Perhaps I should give art college a try. I didn't think

The Twinkle in Pa's Eye

Dad would go for that, though. In any case, it wasn't a passion like the piano, so he might have had the right of it.

I was sitting in the Arboretum one breezy afternoon after school, trying to hold my unplaited hair back with one hand and the paper on my board with the other, when a lady walked out from between some hazel bushes. She stopped for a moment and considered me. I looked down to see if the buttons had come undone on my blouse, or if I had paint on my jeans, but they were okay. So, thinking her very rude, I considered her back.

She was small and very slight, with piercingly blue eyes in a tanned face. She smiled and I swear she could have been a fairy straight out of a children's story. If I blinked, I was sure she'd disappear. She didn't. Instead, she reached into the pocket of her jeans and tied my hair out of my face with a scrunchy.

"How pretty your hair is. I only saw its like once before in my life." She looked wistful. "Do you mind if I sit for a few minutes? I can't stay long."

"Sure." I shifted slightly.

She was wearing a bracelet of small diamonds like dewdrops on a spider's web. She saw me looking and smiled.

"My husband bought it for me before we were married." The lady gazed down at it wistfully and twisted it round and round on her wrist.

She asked if she could look at my sketch. I didn't often share my creations with other people. I didn't think they were good enough.

She took my board on her knee and considered my work carefully.

"Yes, I like it. But it needs a darker color up here to match the weight at the other side. It looks unbalanced."

I was a bit put out. Here was this complete stranger criticizing my work. Who did she think she was? But I took another look, and saw she was absolutely right.

"Thank you." I said grudgingly.

"Please don't be offended. I love art but it's something I have never been any good at. You have a real talent. Well, I have disturbed you long enough. Goodbye Christie."

I was halfway home before I realized she'd called me by name. I hadn't given it to her. I probably imagined it. I pulled the scrunchy from my hair. It glittered like her bracelet.

Chapter Three

Connie Dismayed

Some weeks later I was staying with Auntie Grace again and hammering hell out of her grand. Unlike Mom and Dad, she didn't seem to mind in the least, and occasionally came in with a bagel or a sandwich, which she put on top of the piano..

I was there for three days and on the second day, Auntie Connie arrived. From what I could gather she'd come to get some peace and quiet from her step-daughter.

The minute she saw me the waterworks started again. Darn it, what was wrong with that woman?

"You have turned out so beautiful" she emoted. "Your hair is as gorgeous as I remember." Which was odd as I'd only seen her a couple of months before.

She hugged the breath out of me. I pushed her away and a tear stole down her cheek. Thank God, at that moment, Auntie Grace intervened and said to Auntie Connie:

"We've had breakfast, but I can get something rustled up for you. Plane food is inedible – you must be starving."

"No thanks. But I'd like some coffee. Then, if you don't mind I'd like to rest for a while."

"You're in the usual place. I'll send your coffee up." Grace was looking at me with some concern. Auntie

Connie left.

She snapped: "When she hugs you, it wouldn't kill you to hug her back! I'll cart her off to the library then you can work off your tensions on the piano."

But I was just getting into my stride and had pushed the bench away and stood up like Jerry Lee, when I glanced up and Auntie Connie was standing framed in the doorway. She looked almost gaunt.

"Where did you learn to play like that?" she asked in a toneless voice. I shrugged.

"I didn't really learn. I've always been able to do it."

Grace's head appeared over Connie's left shoulder, and she pulled a face at me to mind my manners.

"Do it again," said Connie, and I launched into a rendition of 'Blueberry Hill'. My singing needed some work. She walked over and stroked my hair because it's a sit-down song.

I felt her stiffen.

"Where did you get that?"

She yanked the scrunchy the lady in the wood had given me from my hair then threw it to the floor as if it had bitten her.

Now who needed a lesson in manners? A chunk of my hair had come away with it.

I explained about the lady I'd met, and after I described her, she ran from the room in hysterics with Grace hot on her heels. I went back to 'Blueberry Hill' but sang louder.

I still couldn't wheedle anything out of Grace. When

I tried, her mouth shut like a trap, and she changed the subject. I was beginning to run out of patience – perhaps Connie would be more forthcoming if I took a slightly different tack.

"What's wrong with the scrunchy? Does it have bugs or something? You hurt me." I added, aggrieved.

"I'm so sorry sweetheart. It looked similar to one I'd seen before. I must have been mistaken. Can I have another look?"

Because I liked it, I'd wound the scrunchy back in my hair, but took it out and handed it to her.

"Sure."

She fingered it then said:

"Did you know these are real diamonds?" I laughed. "They are," Connie insisted. "This is worth a small fortune."

Really, there was no hope for this woman.

The following day, Grace drove me home to Champaign. It was a crisp fall day and the trees in the University quad glimmered gold and russet in the brilliant sunshine. Students were sitting singly or in groups on the lawns, chattering or deeply concentrating.

Dad sat on a bench enjoying a cigarette, as usual with a book balanced on one knee while he drank coffee from a Styrofoam cup. He smiled as Grace pulled up.

"Off you go Christie. I need to speak to your Dad alone for a few minutes," ordered Grace.

She could tell I was annoyed at being dismissed but, typically didn't much care. I dragged my sports bag from the back seat, and set off down the road home, dramatically hefting the bag so they couldn't fail to notice how heavy it was. Such a waste of time.

I never learned what that conversation was about exactly, but the wheels of future events gradually began to turn.

Chapter Four

The Golden Medallion

The first thing that changed was that my visits to the Arboretum were curtailed, and when I was allowed to go someone had to go with me. Mom said it was because she thought it might be dangerous being a young girl alone in the woods. It had never bothered her before.

That meant someone was always looking over my shoulder as I painted, and that I couldn't do. So I was stuck drawing bowls of apples and bottles at the kitchen table.

I did see my lady again once – or at least I think I did. She was walking down the avenue between two rows of overhanging trees. But she didn't see me and was too far away for me to call out.

I was vaguely aware Mom had become very jumpy. She said my piano playing gave her headaches, and even took to yelling at my Dad which left me open-mouthed. He looked a bit put-out too.

One morning, a couple of weeks later, Dad arrived at his study to find a large brown envelope on his desk. Actually, I found it before he did on one of my 'checking-out Dad' expeditions. It had a Texas postmark.

When he found me turning it over in my hands he snatched it away and hid it in his briefcase which he locked.

"What the hell? What's going on Dad? Things around here are getting decidedly weird."

"I can't explain now. We'll talk at home later……and watch your language, young lady."

Young lady? *Young lady?* Who was this guy impersonating my Dad?

Dad must have phoned my Mom because agitation had descended into out-and-out panic. She was wandering around the house wringing her hands and looking as if she'd seen a ghost. I made her three coffees at various stages of the day which she paid scant attention to, before continuing her wandering. Every so often, she would stop and look out of the window as if waiting for someone – I could only assume it was my Dad. I made myself a lunchtime sandwich.

When he finally arrived home, Dad made us all coffee and we sat around the kitchen table. He spread before him the contents of the letter I'd seen that morning and flattened it out with his palms. Texas?

"I have something to tell you which involves us all, but particularly Christie." I was all attention.

"I have been offered a secondment at the University of Texas in Austin."

"Texas?" I said, aghast.

My mother covered her face with her hands.

"There's nothing to panic about. It's a temporary move but will give me experience and opportunities I just can't get here. Given my age, this may be the last offer I'll get."

"But we'll have to move house." said my mother appalled.

"That's true but both Universities will sort out our accommodation. You know that"

"We've lived in this house for twenty years!" said Mom.

If my Dad was trying to be placatory he was failing miserably. Then an appalling thought struck me.

"Grace! Auntie Grace! I won't be able to see her!" I said. Grace would be furious. That should be interesting.

"It's true you won't be able to see her as often. But Auntie Grace is happy for you to stay longer on your visits."

So she was in on it too. My options were shortening.

"But I'll have to start a new school and…..everything!" Any port in a storm - I couldn't care less about school.

"Well, I'm sorry but I'm afraid this is a bit of a 'fait accompli'. It's been under discussion for a month or two and this letter is the acceptance. I have committed to two years with the proviso I get the option to return."

Mom was openly weeping. Her pretty, freckled nose had gone red at the tip. Dad walked round the table and took her in his arms.

"Come on Catherine. You need to be strong. For Christie."

She clung to him. I was shell-shocked. But there

The Twinkle in Pa's Eye

didn't seem to be any point in staying, so I went and barricaded myself in my room to think things through. The end result of my efforts was that if I'd no choice, I might as well accept gracefully.

I found I was absentmindedly winding the lady's scrunchy round my finger. She was the only significant thing that had happened.

Mom and Dad were still in the kitchen and Mom seemed to have pulled herself together. Before they noticed me, Dad said to Mom:

"I defy them to find her there."

Mom blew her nose on a piece of kitchen paper.

Grace drove over to see us before we left and brought Connie with her.

To say there was an atmosphere was putting it mildly. It was clear my Mom and Connie couldn't stand the sight of each other, and as far as I could tell, most of the bad feeling seemed to come from Connie. Grace took me for a coffee for a bit of light relief.

"You know, Connie isn't as bad as you imagine. You've just seen the wrong side of her." said Grace, stirring her mocha.

"Then I've been seeing the wrong side of her for fifteen years."

"Yes, that's true." She looked thoughtful and propped her chin on her hand.

"What it I was to tell you there are things you have yet to learn about Connie."

"I'd say that's the understatement of the century. My entire life's a mystery. I haven't a clue what's happening most of the time."

"Yes, I can see why you would think that. But most of that's teenage-itis. You'll grow out of it."

She finished her coffee and abruptly stood.

"Time to go back."

Grace had neatly sidestepped explaining the Texas debacle, but she wasn't getting away with that. The walk back took fifteen minutes and in that time I managed to drag out of her that the reason we were going was for my own good – oh great, another mystery – and that I should understand the grown-ups in my life had only my best interests at heart. The look on my face quite clearly said it seemed to me the adults in my life didn't know what the hell was going on either.

Grace huffed and strode on ahead, so I'd to run to catch up.

Before they left, Connie took me on one side. She'd dried her eyes and once her face had lost its puffiness, it suddenly struck me how pretty she was. I'd never noticed. She'd an absolutely perfect complexion and her eyes were soft, like a doe's, with long lashes. She wasn't movie-star thin, but slim and shapely and she knew which clothes to wear to accentuate her curves. She could have taught me a thing or two, especially as I had a similar shape but was perhaps a bit too curvy. She smelled of roses.

Connie kissed me gently on the cheek and gave me a loving hug. In her hand she held a little blue velvet box. It contained a small openwork gold pendant on a fine chain. It was a circle with asymmetric lines inside. She fastened it round my neck.

"This was given to me by someone I loved very much. Now I would like you to have it. Keep it close to your heart and think of me sometimes when you wear it."

"I will treasure it. Thank you."

I was dying to ask her who had given it to her, but I didn't want to offend her. It was obviously an item of great sentimental value.

With respect for her love I vowed the only person to unfasten it would be Auntie Connie herself. I would wear it always.

Chapter Five

Off-Track

The move to Austin was relatively painless. Well, relatively without incident anyway.

Before we left, I spent time with Grace, and Connie and Jenny and I said our goodbyes.

I loathed UT on sight. It was a city within a city, modern and sprawling and had none of the charm of Champaign. Our house was one of those built of 'ticky-tacky'. The only thing going for it was its four bedrooms which were quite large. It lacked coziness.

The campus was so big, Dad had a half-mile walk to work. He said it would do him good. Didn't do me good on hot September days, so pretty soon Dad-stalking became a thing of the past.

My school was vast, and I kept getting lost. My fellow students were about as unhelpful as possible. 'Grease' it was not. And my art teachers weren't like those at Champaign. We had life classes with scantily clad ladies with spare tires. No romantic sprigs of blossom or soaring tree branches.

Consequently, my grades plummeted. I spent most of my time alone thinking of Grace and Connie – and Jen, of course. I took to staring out of the window, rubbing Connie's pendant between my fingers or twisting my lady's scrunchy to watch the 'diamonds' glitter. I was sad and so alone.

I wrote frequent letters to Grace which she was punctilious about answering. I asked her for Connie's address, but she said it would be better to send any letters to her, and she would forward them. Saved on the postage, I supposed.

There was one, temporary light in the darkness. I met this boy. His name was Ian Beecham. He was a first-year chemistry student so a couple of years older than me. But he had wild curly hair which he wore pushed back off his face, and a rather straggly beard.

All the girls mooned over him, but for some reason best known to himself he seemed to have taken a shine to me. We had a friendship which my parents were pleased about as I'd made no other effort in that direction.

There was a cannabis café on campus and Ian took me there once or twice, although being under eighteen I wasn't supposed to go. At first, I was scared, and just looked about at the chatter and happy vibe. After a while curiosity overcame my scruples, and I tried it. It did much to lighten my mood. It had different effects on different people, I found. Me, it made giggly and Ian amorous. Not a good combination.

So, being as high as kites made our romance blossom faster than it should have, and certainly faster than was good for me. He would chase me across the lawns and pull me to the ground where we lay panting and laughing.

Without me noticing, he began to search out more

private areas of the campus and of course, eventually the inevitable happened. It was lovely. So we smoked some more and did it again. I wasn't stupid. I saw the doctor and began taking the pill.

My parents noticed the change in me, although I was careful not to go home high or let the smell give me away.

Had I been older and more experienced I would have known there were two ways this relationship could go. Either we could take something stronger or end it. Although it broke my heart, I decided to say goodbye.

So I was alone again and more miserable than ever. My parents packed me off to stay with Grace. I was so relieved I cried.

I said somewhere there was something of the psychic about Grace. I swear I said not one word, but she knew I'd been up to something. It didn't take her long to wheedle it out of me. She was better at that kind of thing than I could ever hope to be.

"Well, if you want my opinion, which I am absolutely certain you don't – but which you're going to get anyway - I'd say it's time you found something else to think about."

"Like what? I've tried lots of stuff."

"So I noticed," she said dryly. "If you don't like your art teacher – you're probably better than he is anyway – why don't you have a word with your Dad and use his influence to join the University Art Society? Also, you could boogie-woogie your way into a band. But judging by past events you might still be too juvenile for that kind of thing."

Juvenile…. JUVENILE! There is nothing in this world a teenager hates more than being told she's immature. Grace could rattle my keys like I could play the piano. Right! That was it! Band it was then.

Chapter Six

Singing the Blues

Once home again, I set about following Grace's advice. It wasn't as easy as I thought. I was sixteen and could pass for…. sixteen. So no checking out the student bar, and no way was I going back to the cannabis club.

This time I embarked on it the intelligent way and asked my Dad for help. He was very anti at first, but I persuaded him into putting out some feelers for me. Although only Grace had guessed at my misdemeanors, both Dad and Mom knew I hadn't settled in well. In the end, it was Mom who finally talked him round.

"At least it'll get her out of the house, and I can get my hearing back. Maybe even have a few friends round. She'll have fun!"

I had a feeling the last was less important than what came before, but perhaps that was unfair. My mother loved me deeply, but I was a teenager and even I knew that could be trying.

Eventually, I met up with a girl called Eve Nixon who was in her Master's year, so a lot older than me. She managed one of the University bands.

She agreed to an audition, and I was ushered onto a dim stage with the oldest, most battered piano I'd ever seen in my life. I just hoped all the keys worked or I was in trouble.

I tentatively pressed down middle C, then F# followed by A. The timbre was wonderful. There would be little need for pedals which for someone who liked to play standing up was a definite advantage. I spread my fingers across the keys and tried a couple of chords. That was it. I was lost to the world as I played the opening bars of a Floyd Cramer number. I was just morphing into Crocodile Rock when I felt – couldn't hear a thing – a banging on the stage.

"Okay, okay. You've proved your point," Eve was grinning all over her face. "That's rock n roll. How's your blues?"

"Don't know. Never tried. I play by ear so I can't think it would be difficult to pick up if someone shows me."

"Good answer. I'll fix that."

It was then that I became aware of a figure standing at the back of the hall. He was in the shadows so I could only see that he was quite short.

"Who's that?." I asked Eve. I'd thought we were alone and was a bit put out that she might have brought someone else along without telling me.

"Who?" she said and spun round. But by this time the figure had disappeared.

"Did you bring someone with you?" I accused. She looked puzzled.

"I certainly did not. I would have told you if I had."

When I got home, I told my parents about the audition but didn't mention the stranger in the shadows.

Eve had told me if I could handle the blues numbers, I was in. She offered to send someone round to the house to give me a bit of instruction. Would that be acceptable? Sure would!

When the guy turned up the following evening, I could have sworn it was the person from the theatre.

He was forty-ish - perhaps a little younger - small, with a vaguely oriental cast to his features. He introduced himself as Bobby.

As Eve had done, he started off by asking me to play a little something. 'Great Balls of Fire' was always impressive.

When I'd finished, he looked shocked at the ferocity of my delivery. There was a significant pause then he said:

"Wow!" He looked lost for words.

"Bit loud?" I asked.

"No. Not in the least. You can't have quiet rock n roll. I was just a little shocked that such a little lady could make so much noise."

He started to laugh which went some way to smoothing the hackles raised by his sexist remark. He continued:

"You're going to have to tone it down a lot for blues, though."

Bobby sat on the bench and drew from the keys the most sublime sound I'd ever heard. Lots of sharps and flats, I noticed, but it reminded me of a poem I'd once had to learn at school, which until that moment I'd never fully understood:

"I chatter over stony ways
In little sharps and trebles
I bubble into eddying bays
I babble on the pebbles."

It was fluid one moment and direct the next. I just loved it. It made my playing seem brash.

"Come and sit by me."

He arranged his fingers on the lower registers of the keyboard and told me to copy on the top notes.

"There's a technique to it. You have the skill to learn it quite easily, but you need to reel it right in. Learn to be quiet."

His fingers trilled across the keys moving from major to minor and back again.

"You try."

My first attempt? Well, let's just say Memphis Slim's crown was secure.

"Try again," said Bobby. "A little sweeter. Run the notes together smoothly like this."

After an hour, Bobby shook my father's hand and bowed his head respectfully at my mother. He left two albums for me to listen to and try to copy.

We had another couple of lessons by which time I was becoming reasonably competent but that was all.

The Twinkle in Pa's Eye

I can only imagine the quality of the other applicants because, after hearing my efforts with blues numbers, Eve agreed to keep me on and introduced me to the other band members.

I was pleased to see the lead singer was a girl, so I wouldn't be on my own. She called herself Deedee but I rather think her name was Diane. This little bit of posing aside, she seemed to be okay – friendly, in fact. Perhaps she was relieved to have another girl in the band.

She was very pretty with long, strawberry blonde hair with a natural curl and spectacular eye-makeup. Also, tall and stick thin which I hated her for. She was naturally the mic-hugging blues singer type but could also do a raunchy rock number.

The lead guitarist was called Jez. He seemed incapable of playing a horizontal instrument. When on stage, his guitar neck was either pointing up to the ceiling or down to the floor. He had shoulder-length hair and wore sunglasses – shades, man – which seemed glued to his nose.

The bass player, Frank Jones, I liked. He was a little ginger-haired guy with a quiet confident manner.

The drummer thought he was Jamie Robson. Arms and legs all over the place and a great deal of sweat. His name was Phil Taylor.

I seemed to slot right in, sweat apart. I was given a friendly welcome which increased when they'd heard me play. As I hammered away, they joined in a great jam session which turned out some pretty good stuff. I slipped into blues chords with trepidation, but once they joined in, it lifted my confidence, and I began to feel a natural affinity for the music.

Eve gave me a set list and some tapes of the band and walked home with me. She told me when I thought I had the hang of it, we'd all get together for rehearsals.

She needed a signature on a release form because I was under-age. My mother read it and signed it without comment. My father, who would have been more particular, was at work.

I practiced manically.

I wrote to Grace to keep her informed. If she was impressed by my superstar status, she didn't let on. Instead, she wrote a long tedious letter about her holiday home in San Clemente on the Californian coast. She'd see Auntie Connie and Oliver while she was there and did I have any messages.

She made passing reference to my newly acquired skills at the blues and asked if someone had taught me or I'd figured it out for myself like the rock n roll. I told her about Bobby. She didn't mention him at all in her return letter. Seemed little, polite and oriental didn't cut it with Auntie G.

The big day of my first gig arrived. Not locking myself in the lavatory took some doing.

In the scheme of things, it was no big deal – Eve had been thoughtful enough to start me off gently. We were due to play for an hour in the refectory during a formal dinner. Hardly mind-bending stuff but perhaps if they clattered the cutlery loudly enough, no-one would hear my mistakes. When I said as much to Deedee she nearly choked on her gum. Jez looked over his shades and said:

"Hey man, be cool."

Which set both of us off. Being cool was so not fun.

It went off without a hitch. Mostly, I suspect, because nobody was listening. I caught sight of my Dad for a brief moment across the room. He appeared to be chatting with Bobby. It was hard to tell because all the men were wearing the same get-up. By comparison their partners looked like peacocks.

Eve came by afterwards and slapped twenty-five bucks each in our hands. I am sometimes unbelievably dim. It had never occurred to me once I'd be getting paid.

Jez and Phil had their heads together muttering. Odd words were audible.

"…..bastards……best…..only a twenty……. next time." or something of the sort.

Bobby came to congratulate me on my first appearance. He'd taken off his bow tie and opened his shirt collar to cool off. I didn't see my Dad.

My conversation with Bobby wasn't long as Jez kept flicking rolled up cigarette papers at my head. But I thanked him very much for all his help and asked if he would like to pay us another visit at home. 'Ping'. He couldn't, he said apologetically, as he was due to fly out to somewhere in the 'ping' mid-West – don't remember where – early in the morning.

He bent his head to kiss my hand 'ping' and, as he did so, a small gold shape on a chain dangled free of his open shirt-collar. With the briefest of glances, 'ping' it looked exactly the twin of the one Connie had given me. I must have been mistaken. I wore mine all the time and Bobby must have seen it often but never mentioned it. Surely he would have.

So I opened my mouth and put both feet in it

"Jez, give me that freakin' catapult, you childish bastard." I blushed red as a beet and clapped my hands to my mouth.

"Oh, Bobby, please forgive me. I'm a complete ass."

I cringed again. There was no getting out of this gracefully, so as he dropped my hand I asked:

"Can I see your pendant Bobby?"

He took it off and held it in the palm of his hand. I peered at it and pushed it around with my finger. No doubt at all. It was an exact duplicate of my own. I showed him the chain around my neck.

I was amazed he didn't appear in the least surprised.

"Christians wear a cross. I have one too on the same chain. See? And members of my church wear this symbol"

"My Aunt Connie – Connie Maxwell - gave this to me. She said it had been given to her by someone she once cared a lot about. Do you know her?"

Now wouldn't that have been a coincidence. How idiotic can you get?

"Aunt Connie I don't personally know, sadly." The

words seemed carefully chosen. "If she wore this symbol she is likely to be a lady worth knowing, so the loss is mine."

He smiled his gentle smile and turned to leave. I put my hand on his arm.

"I would like to thank you so much for your patience. You have taught me so much."

I realized with a start that I was saying goodbye to him, probably for always. It was a very unwelcome thought. He looked deep into my eyes and said softly.

"Don't be sad, Christie. I promise you we will meet again."

I was sorry Bobby and I parted so suddenly because there was no opportunity to grill him further on the pendant. Perhaps Grace had some insight. But for the first time ever in my whole lifetime, on this one subject, I truly believed she hadn't a clue.

Chapter Seven

Angel

All that summer the gigs continued. As I got better, I enjoyed them more. Deedee became a special friend and a sharer of mischief – mostly harmless. Jez became a pain in the ass. He seemed bent on doing absolutely anything at all to annoy me. Oh boy, did he manage that!

My schoolwork was mediocre, but I didn't care and unusually, my parents seemed too preoccupied in other directions to be bothered. Mom had joined a Bridge club, of all things, and had made a whole bunch of new friends in the process. Dad was in the middle of moderating exams.

I turned seventeen that December, just before Christmas.

I awoke bright and early to open gifts and cards. Mom brought me breakfast in bed and jumped up and down excitedly as I opened everything. What the hell had gotten into her?

It did occur to me as strange that Dad hadn't been there when I opened my presents. He was always there. Mom was still behaving strangely and kept running upstairs and staring at the street. I shrugged and made her a coffee.

Then Dad rushed through the door, University scarf flying and the biggest grin I ever saw stretched across his face. He grabbed my arm.

"Come on, come on, come on!" he said, and dragged me to the door.

There, parked on the curb, was what must have been the ugliest car to ever hit the production line. It was an AMC Pacer in brick red. Dad dangled the keys in my face. I grabbed them and opened up this particular birthday box. I absolutely loved it on sight. Ugly car it may have been, but it was *my* ugly car. All mine – my own wheels.

Of course, there was only one thing missing. I couldn't drive. But I was a seventeen-year-old kid in America, for God's sake. I'd been driving my Dad's car - first sat on his knee - then when I was big enough taking instruction from him, since I was ten. He'd no doubt at all I'd get my drivers' license first time round. I was pretty sure myself.

I spent every moment I could muster between school and gigs in driving with my Mom or Dad. The only problem I had was backing into a space. That blew it for supermarket parking, but I could live with that, I thought. That was hardly the point though so I worked and worked to get it right and…. I passed first time. I photocopied my drivers' license and framed it on my bedroom wall.

Of course, there are draw-backs to being in a band, and having your own wheels was one of them, as I very quickly found out. I was bullied into carting people and instruments to gigs, until Phil's drum pedal ripped a hole in my back seat. That was it – no more instruments and only as many people as there were seat belts for – the last came as an order from Grace.

After that travelling got easier. Phil and Frank couldn't afford to run a car – tuition fees were terrifying for them. Jez had a car, but it was a law unto itself. Sometimes it worked and sometimes it didn't. Not even the local garage could discover why. Deedee said it was because he pissed it off. She was probably right.

Because we could now get about easier, Eve was able to book gigs further out. Still nothing thrilling but we could travel to San Antonio and even Houston at a push. We were still playing mostly Universities, but I could see we were getting quite a fan following. I even had a guy get hold of my ankle and try to pull me off stage. Jez stood on his hand.

We played a whole series of Saturday night gigs at the San Antonio campus.

Not to be conceited or anything, but I was getting pretty good. I really began to appreciate the blues and Deedee improved along with me. We did at one point think of ditching the guys and doing our own thing, but it wouldn't have been as much fun. Besides, they did most of the hefting, which was okay for her, but I'd have had a problem.

We were packing up from the last show in San Antonio when I happened to glance into the wings. I looked closer. A delicate hand with a glimmering band at its wrist was holding back the curtain. The rest of her was in shadow so I couldn't make her out, but the scent of gardenias was unmistakable.

I dropped what I was doing and ran. But by the time I grabbed at the curtain she was gone, although her perfume lingered.

My hand strayed to my pendant and I rubbed it between my thumb and finger. I had to get a look at that woman. If she was wearing the same pendant as Bobby and me, they had to know each other. Anything else would be too much of a coincidence.

Once back in Austin, I dropped Deedee off then pelted into the University library and leafed through the books on religion – emphasis on 'hippie' - to check out that symbol. I couldn't find it at first then flicked over a page about some cult in Los Angeles. It was a product of 'flower power' but seemed to have soaked up a number of celebs who no doubt kept it afloat with contributions. There was a quarter page image of my medallion – it was unmistakable. Amongst the adherents was a handful of famous actresses and pop stars I recognized, including Gil Robson. But they were all big in the sixties so pretty old by now.

How this concerned Connie, I didn't know. Perhaps it didn't. Perhaps it just concerned the person who had given it to her. I'd ask Grace when next I visited.

The awful truth was that I hadn't seen Grace for months since we moved to Austin. I felt very guilty without quite knowing why. It wasn't as if she was some lonely old lady who spent her time doing charity work and arranging flowers. She was bright, lively and interested in everything.

I called her and asked if it would be okay for me to come and spend a whole week at Spring break. I was still in love with my old jalopy and really wanted to drive to Windham, but my Dad put his foot down, backed firmly by Grace. It was over a thousand miles through some poor areas of Oklahoma. I wasn't scared but I could see they were nervous, so I agreed to fly. Grace would pick me up at O'Hare in Chicago.

Grace met me at the pick-up area out front of the airport. Connie was with her.

I was so thrilled to see them both I couldn't stop chattering. About nothing in particular and about everything in the world.

I saw Connie's eyes drop to the neckline of my shirt and, once she'd located the pendant, she smiled up at me with real affection and I mouthed a 'thank you' when Grace turned away. I'd become aware of how important a gift it was to her and wondered why she had decided to part with it.

Chapter Eight
Enter Apollo

The days passed in indolent pleasure. We had a day shopping in Chicago then I drove Grace's car to Jackson Park, where we walked amongst trees which reminded me of the Arboretum in Champaign. It seemed to me that between them, Grace and Connie completely replaced my wardrobe. I let them. They were clearly having a ball, but naturally I looked like their version of Christie and not necessarily my own.

One morning, Grace was busy in her office on the phone, and Connie and I took a walk in the extensive gardens, down gravel paths lined with magnificent rhododendrons. It was then I finally got the chance to ask her about the medallion.

"I saw someone in Austin with exactly the same pendant you gave me. A man who taught me piano. Was there a reason for that? Did you know him?"

"Well, I don't think so. It's not likely. It's an international movement so he could have been anyone."

I'd known her all my life, so when she turned her head away, I knew it wasn't true. I took another tack which really was the crux of the matter.

"Who gave the pendant to you? You said it was a special person."

I tried, and failed, to look nonchalant so I was surprised when she didn't block me again.

"My husband."

"You said it was someone you loved."

"Yes, there is a part of me that always will. I wish it wasn't so, but it is."

She looked so crestfallen.

"Please don't discuss this with Grace. She is such a wonderful friend to me. I wouldn't like to hurt her."

Of course, Grace knew. Grace could figure anything out. But I kept that thought to myself because I was sure Connie already knew it too.

"My husband was probably the finest person I have ever known, but we didn't fit. We should have known that from the start. Please, Christie, I'd rather not discuss this anymore."

There was no point in pushing her further. She'd already told me more than she wanted to.

I put my arm round her shoulders and we returned to the house, silent.

The following morning, I returned to Austin.

I sat in my room and felt bereft. Mom understood. She knew how much I loved Grace. I was left alone and never questioned by either of my parents. I thought that was very tactful of them.

I mooched about for the couple of days before the new semester began. I took my sketch book. I was older now and spent hours alone, drawing like I had as a kid. I often thought of my lady walking amongst the hazels and sitting next to me on the tree stump. My memory of her seemed so elusive. Perhaps she'd been the wood nymph I'd taken her for.

One day, I tried to capture what I could remember of her features on my pad, but the only part of her I remembered clearly was the delicate hand with the diamond bracelet. Strangely, I could remember every single stone, but not the eyes which had smiled into mine.

On my last day of freedom, I was astounded to see her in the street near the math block, chatting to Bobby who I thought had left town long ago. When they saw me, the lady slipped quietly away, but Bobby greeted me with a welcoming smile.

"Hi Christie. How did the gigs go? I understand you stole the show."

"Who was the lady you were talking to?"

I was so intent on finding who she was, I forgot my manners completely. But he wasn't in the least fazed.

"Oh, Giulia? She's just an acquaintance of my sister's."

I must have got it wrong – after all I'd met her in Illinois and that was years ago.

"May I hear how your playing is progressing? Are you free for me to call round this evening?" asked Bobby, changing the subject abruptly.

"Sure."

I knew there was something going on here and had known since I first saw Giulia in the Arboretum years ago. I'd get this out of Bobby if it killed me.

He called around six-thirty and changed our plans. He couldn't make it he said, but could we re-arrange for Saturday afternoon.

The band had practice Saturday, so I asked the guys if he could sit in with us, maybe play a little piano if they didn't mind. They hadn't a clue who he was, and it suddenly struck me, neither did I. Odd that - I just knew him as a polite guy who played piano and wore a pendant. I suspected he also hung around in dark halls watching a bunch of people he'd never met before, which was a bit creepy.

He gave off the vibe of being a professional, so the guys buckled down to work, a bit like naughty kids caught by the teacher. It was funny watching Jez play his guitar horizontally, and Phil trying to play drums like Hal Blaine rather than Jamie Robson.

At one point Deedee had her fist stuffed in her mouth and tears running down her face. But she pulled herself together pronto when it came to singing. She'd a powerful voice and her pièce de resistance was Billie Holiday's 'Lover Man', which I always thought was terminally depressing. But the audience liked it and that was what counted.

Bobby seemed to like it too. He asked if he could take over piano while she sang. I must admit to being a bit put out but shrugged and moved aside anyway.

I learned more about playing piano in those five minutes than I had since I'd known him. He sent the rest of them off for a coke and showed me some of the intricacies of technique he'd used. The effects, even with my lack of experience, were magical. I swore never to play rock n roll again.

He seemed impressed I could follow him. To tell the truth, he wasn't the only one. But it did kinda leave me with a problem because I couldn't now ask him to the house for another lesson. And he was too old to invite on a date – he must have been forty if he was a day. It went against every inclination I had but there was only one other option. When we were alone, I asked Deedee:

"Can you invite Bobby to the next gig?"

"Invite him yourself. Why ask me? Anyway, he's a bit elderly, isn't he?"

"He is, but he plays cool piano, and I want to study how he plays. I need to hear him with your voice."

She looked flattered. Had she realized I just wanted to know where his necklace came from, she might have been less impressed.

Although I still had hopes of listening to Bobby play piano on stage with Deedee, it turned out not to be such an issue.

On the evening of my first day at school, the doorbell rang. Bobby had been passing and had just dropped in to say goodbye to my parents. Not a word to me. He couldn't stay. He was due to leave town because he was on tour in the Mid-West.

Ah-ha! Another bit of information to squirrel away. He played in a band good enough to do national tours. I didn't recognize him but there was no saying he was a lead. He might even have been a roadie, although it would have been a waste of a piano player.

I would get to the bottom of this. I realized I kept saying the same thing, but I was making absolutely no progress.

That same evening, my Dad sat me down in the sitting-room and looked all serious. Oh Lord, please not again.

"I hope you will agree to be adult about what I am about to say, Christie," not hopeful, "because some of it you won't agree with. I want you to know I am well aware of this before I begin."

Oh hell, were they sending me to a correctional institution? All I did was smoke a bit of pot and play piano underage in Uni bars.

"Oh…. not like that!" he said, rather impatiently, I thought. "This is your final year at school, and you need to put in some major work if you are to graduate. Your science and Spanish grades, especially, are dreadful and you need to really buckle down."

What a relief. I knew all this. I'd bummed around all year and missed classes but played pretty good piano. That made up for it a bit, didn't it? Apparently no, it did not.

"For this reason, for the time being at least, you are to quit the band and give schoolwork your full attention"

WHAT! I looked to see even a glimmer of amusement in his eyes. All I saw was determination. My life was over. Without another word I stalked off to my room.

The Twinkle in Pa's Eye

If I was expecting sympathy, I was sorely disappointed. I finally emerged when I began to feel faint from hunger. I ate, then mooched around the house until bedtime, trying to illicit sympathy from someone, anyone. No dice.

The following morning, I was packing my school bag when the phone rang. It was Grace. Oh, God….it was Grace. What had they told her now?

The dressing-down she gave me could have been heard in Arizona. I was to pick myself up, stop feeling sorry for myself and get the hell on with my schoolwork. Bands were for people without brains who could do nothing else.

I went to school walking off my anger rather than taking the bus. I arrived late and got detention.

That day, also, I was given my schedule for the year. It was appalling. I could finally see how there was no way I could do all this work and still be in the band. I didn't think that was right. What kind of school did away with extra-curricular activities? Granted it was hardly chess or volleyball but then I didn't want to be a teacher, so surely studying for what I did want to do should be the right thing.

When I mentioned my reasoning to my music teacher, I was told you had to be exceptional to be a professional musician and then you needed a whole ton of luck. I'd a feeling Bobby was the latter. And anyway, all she taught was the Beethoven stuff so she'd no idea at all what I could do.

I sat in the Arboretum and cried in frustration. Then I

had to go home before they set the police on me.

As I ran down the sidewalk, I bumped into someone, and the books from my bag flew everywhere. Some pages came loose and fluttered down the road. Oh hell, if this wasn't just the end. I should go to the top of the Math block and throw myself off so my Dad could watch me splatter.

The person I'd charged into had stopped to help me pick everything up and pack them back in my bag. Then the sun came out.

He was an old guy. Maybe the same as Bobby, but he'd an agelessness about his tall, slim frame. With shining blonde hair which reached his shoulders he reminded me of a Greek god we'd learned about in grade school. He wore the same type of round wire-rimmed glasses favored by John Lennon. All in all, he was pretty spectacular. I stared, then collected myself and remembered I was supposed to be picking my books up.

"I am so sorry" I gasped. "I'm late going home so I was running."

How lame could you get!

"So I see" he grinned. I blushed to the roots of my hair. "Bad day?"

"Oh, the worst. First day of my final year and so much work I've had to pack in my band."

Why the hell was I telling him this?

"You play in a band? Which instruments do you play?"

Instruments plural? Might as well go along with it. He didn't know if I was telling a fib and I wouldn't see him again anyway. I'd said the same about my lady of the Arboretum but I'd seen her since – connected to Bobby, also mysterious.

"Keyboards mostly." I said nonchalantly. By this time all the books were back in my bag, so I was feeling marginally better. "I can do rock but I really prefer blues. Billie Holliday stuff in particular."

"I'm impressed" he said without the glimmer of a smile. "Do you sing then?"

"Sure"

My voice would knock holes in the Hoover Dam.

He bent down to pick up a stray pencil I'd dropped. As he did so a chain dropped from his shirt and glistened in the sunshine. Oh God, not again. This was getting beyond a joke. But it was only a small gold cross. I sighed a breath of relief.

He handed me the pencil. The symbol was hanging from a leather strap around his wrist.

"Thanks" I said, taking the pencil. I disappeared down the road at a rate of knots.

Chapter Nine

No Pain No Gain

I went to see the guys to give them my bad news.

They weren't surprised. Eve was taking her finals. My friend Deedee had moved away without telling me. Her father was also a lecturer and had moved to another university somewhere in California. She'd love that. She'd fit right in.

Jez was also in his final school year. No doubt his father had laid the law down too.

Frank and Phil were still around, but what good were drums and a bass without the others?

The rest of the year was depressing. My Dad kept my nose to the grindstone by helping me with my nightly homework. He did want to help but I knew it was mostly to keep me focused.

And – hallelujah! – I did finally graduate. Life could begin again! Now I could get on with the major job of convincing the world I was a rock star and not an accountant or, perish the thought, a lawyer.

Grace and Connie came down that weekend for the celebration. I was so delighted to see them.

Dad had booked a restaurant a couple of months before. Naturally, all the restaurants would be filled with other celebrations for other students. He must have had more faith in my abilities than I'd thought.

The restaurant was okay as even Grace approved of the menu, which was mostly in French. She ordered for me, thank goodness.

Connie and my mother sat as far away from each other as they could. Everybody loved everybody in our family, so I found it hard to fathom why they would avoid eye contact. Connie seemed to spend a lot of time examining the occupants of other tables.

While Dad was paying the bill, the man I'd knocked into that afternoon walked in, with a very pretty lady with waist-length blonde hair and a maxi skirt.

He grinned and waved at me, tipping his head slightly to the others at the table. I waved back and turned to pick up my purse from the floor. As I lifted my head I saw Connie, who was sitting across from me, was as stiff as a board and ashen faced. I took a quick look about me but, apart from the couple who had just arrived, nothing else had changed.

Perhaps she was unwell. Grace must have come to the same conclusion as she raised her by the arm and carted her off to the restroom, smiling at everyone for both of them. As they walked off I heard her say to Connie:

"Who was that? LA?" Connie nodded.

They had been due to take the evening plane the following day, but Grace asked if it would be okay for them to stop on for another day to allow Connie, who still looked ghastly, to recuperate. My mother looked less than enthusiastic but didn't refuse. Another jolly day in the offing.

The following day, Saturday, Grace took Connie out to look round Austin and do some shopping. Mom and I weren't invited which was no big deal, since it meant I could hammer the piano for an hour or two. Mom couldn't stand the sight of Connie anyway, and Dad was in his office at work.

After a while, my arms and legs felt stiff from sitting at the piano – I sat when I wasn't being Jerry Lee - so I piled my hair on top of my head, secured it with a scrunchy, pulled on my joggers and set off for the park. It was a beautiful day. Bright trees against emerald grass. I ran across the campus and through a little park area where students were laughing and fooling about on the lawns. Little artificial streams gurgled under miniature bridges. All was right with the world.

I stopped to talk with some kids from school and we drank from flasks and dangled our hot toes in the cool water, until a park warden moved us on. Then we parted ways and I continued my run. I cut off the tarmac to enjoy the dappled sunlight of the gardens. Complete strangers waved at me from the windows of a university block. It was that kind of day.

As I neared the wrought iron gates which closed off the park to the public at night, I heard a lot of shouting and was shoved to the ground by a boy with a police officer in hot pursuit. I fell on my left arm which folded underneath me.

The chase continued, and the officer pulled a gun yelling at the bystanders to get down, but the perpetrator got away.

I was left in their wake, leaning sideways on my knees unable to move a muscle from the agonizing pain which shot up my arm.

A couple of guys tried to help me to my feet, but I screamed so loud I must have frightened the shit out of them. Then a saint in the guise of a rotund, elderly lady yelled at them to stop and call a medic. A commanding voice told her to mind her own business.

I was sobbing into the tarmac, trying to move my arm into a more comfortable position and failing miserably. I screamed again.

I was so desperately grateful when the strident voice turned out to be Auntie Grace's. Oh God, she was a sight for sore eyes.

Or perhaps not. She grabbed hold of my arm and yanked as hard as she could. I screamed and screamed. There was a clearly audible snap as the dislocated bone resited itself.

I vomited into a waste bin from the pain. I'd to sit down for a full five minutes. But although sore, my arm was at least functioning again.

Connie kept out of the way while all this was happening. I guess she was afraid of doing more harm than good. When things began to settle down a bit, she emerged from behind a park bench, took my face in her hands and kissed my forehead.

"Oh my sweetheart, are you alright? Is there anything I can do? Her soft eyes were predictably, filled with tears which clung to her lashes, then splashed unbidden against her lace camisole. She rubbed her forehead against mine, afraid to touch me in case she caused me pain.

"I'll go fetch the car round" said Grace, practical as ever. "You…. whatever your name is…. Get her to the gate anyway you can. God-damn one-way systems!"

She walked off rattling her keys and cursing the local authorities.

I was surprised to see she'd been talking to the man who had helped pick up my books earlier in the day. He was standing slightly behind Connie and with all the upset, I hadn't noticed him.

Grace threw her Liberty scarf at him as she passed. Apparently, although she didn't say so, to temporarily strap up my arm.

Connie held my shoulders still while he, light-fingered, strapped my arm across my chest. It was still agony but not gut-wrenching as before.

"Do you think you could walk, or do you need me to carry you?"

I glanced at his slender arms, I hoped covertly, and decided I'd rather walk.

We met Grace at the gates – she'd driven the wrong way up a one-way street – and he gently folded me into the front seat of Grace's hire car and shut the door. I gave him a wobbly smile of gratitude. Connie jumped in the back.

Grace did a U-turn – was she trying to get us killed?

– and headed for home.

"The hospital's the other way" I said, confused.

"You're not going to hospital, dear. You only dislocated your elbow. It'll fix in a day or two once the swelling goes down, if you keep it still."

When you were in dire need of comfort, her practicality could sometimes grate. I could tell Connie agreed with me from the gasp from the back seat. So, I played the invalid as best I could in her direction and groaned as we went over a bump in the road. Grace glared at me.

"Where's the man who helped us?" I asked, suddenly remembering. I wasn't so debilitated I forgot I wanted to know who he was.

"Who was he? Can I find him to thank him?"

Grace shrugged but Connie said:

"His name was Harry but that's all I remember."

Crap! Another opportunity lost.

When we got home, I began to be grateful for Grace's reticence. My mother was all over me like a rash. She barged Connie out of the way and supported me up the stairs to bed, all the while asking questions I couldn't be bothered to answer. She could grill someone else. Probably not Connie whose face was like thunder.

I sank onto my bed, drank a glass of warm milk which appeared, with a couple of paracetamols, out of nowhere, and slept off the shock. As I drifted off, I was vaguely aware of a lot of hollering from downstairs.

The Twinkle in Pa's Eye

I dreamed of an Apollo with wire-rimmed specs and thin arms who morphed, strangely, into someone else. He had soft, cloud-blue eyes and the sweetest smile I ever saw. But I didn't know who he was.

Chapter Ten

What's With Mom?

Grace called the police and made sure the perpetrator, when caught, was charged with actual bodily harm, before she set off home.

My mother lifted Grace's luggage into the trunk, leaving Connie to cope with her own in the hall.

She was crying again. Big surprise.

I kissed them both and hugged them tightly, promising to visit as soon as I could.

I was very angry with my Mom. She'd done nothing at all to mend fences with Connie, one of the people I'd relied on in an emergency. She should be grateful to her. Instead, she was behaving as if Connie was the enemy. There could be no excuse for that. When I told her so, she looked guilty and left the room.

My Dad sided with Grace. No permanent harm had been done. We should be grateful for small mercies. I decided he was right.

A few weeks later, Dad came back from work with a familiar-looking brown envelope. Again, he opened it in front of us at the kitchen table. We waited with bated breath.

Oooeee! We were going back to Illinois. I had a car now so I could see Grace any time I liked. What if she got sick of the sight of me?

When I got more used to it, now I was eighteen, they'd

have to let me drive.

Perhaps I could even get to visit Connie. I'd never been to LA. No way would I want to do that journey by car though. That would be a couple of days – and through Oklahoma which Dad would never allow. Amtrak was even worse but by plane from Chicago it was only a few hours direct.

But that was just a fleeting thought for the future. For now, I was going home, and I couldn't be more delighted. Despite Dad's promises at the start, his contract term of two years had almost doubled. My mother just wanted her old house back.

First there was a school year to complete which included the dreaded SATs. My Dad thought I hadn't a hope in hell of doing anything useful. Well, I'd just have to prove him wrong. Of course, he could be using reverse psychology, but I couldn't be sure.

My mother thought I'd make a reasonable housewife and set about teaching me to bake with the obvious outcome. Anyone who could hammer a piano keyboard was hardly likely to be good at pastry.

The year saw its ups and downs – towards the end, mostly downs as I started to dread my Dad had been right. But I did pretty well although my Dad looked down his nose at me and threatened resits and private tuition. Ha! Who did he think he was kidding? I'd run away from home first!

Connie just hugged me and said: "Well done, darling.

I knew you could do it." Thank God for Connie.

Connie suggested, as a reward for my hard work – even I laughed – I should come and spend a week with her in California. I thought that was the best ever idea. We could go and see her mother in Santa Monica, she said. She would take me round Hollywood, then Grace could meet us at her holiday place in San Clemente. Sounded just about perfect. Grace gave the plan the thumbs-up.

I was a bit surprised therefore, that when the idea was mooted to my mother, she stormed out of the house in a temper of hysterics, slamming the door behind her. My Dad looked shell-shocked. When she hadn't come home after an hour, he got in his car and began trawling the streets to find her.

I pulled on my jean-jacket and trainers and set off on foot. I'd a vague idea of where she'd be. There was a narrow stream in the University grounds, overhung with willows. Beside it was a rustic wooden bench, almost hidden from the path by branches which arched gracefully down to touch the water.

She was there, sobbing into a soggy tissue.

I sat on the bench next to her. I was at a loss. What should I say to her? So I did the obvious and handed her the little pack of tissues I always carried with me. At least they were dry.

Eventually, she blew her nose and said:

"Come on, let's go home. Dad will be worried."

"He's out searching the streets of Austin. He's

convinced you've jumped off a bridge, or something. So what's the problem, anyway?"

"Oh, I was just so concerned about you travelling all that way alone. You've never been further away than from Windham to Champaign on your own. Los Angeles is on the other side of the Continent."

"Oh, is that all?" I countered. "That's no problem. I've asked Auntie Connie to take me back next time she comes to see Grace"

My mother fainted. I mean, fainted and was lying flat out on the ground. What the hell did I do now?

Fortunately, a jogger came to my aid and helped me hoist her back onto the bench, unceremoniously pushed her head between her knees and handed me a bottle of water. Then he continued on his way. He must have known what he was doing because within ten minutes, she was good to go.

I'd expected my Dad to baby her as he usually did but he was absolutely furious.

He yelled at me to get upstairs and not to come down until he said so. Then to my absolute astonishment, he laid into my poor mother at full throttle.

I went upstairs and turned the sound to full on my deck.

Chapter Eleven

Atom Bomb in Champaign

Periodically, I turned down my music. Gradually, the furore diminished. Then there was a loud rap on my door and my Dad walked in. He was stony faced, and I was afraid for a moment I was going to get the same treatment he'd doled out to poor Mom.

All he said was:

"Please come down, Christie. We have a matter to discuss with you. You will please excuse your mother. She is not rational on this subject, but it is something she has always known she would have to face sooner or later. That time is now."

Oh…my…. God! Did I have some incurable disease which would mean I could die at any time? Was somebody else going to die? Grace? Connie? My mother?

Coffee was laid out on the kitchen table with a plate of ham sandwiches. A long session then. I was beginning to feel my stomach churn.

"Now you are eighteen years old and have completed your school education, your mother and I have decided," - she looked as if she wanted no part of this at all - "it's time we told you things which can only be addressed to an adult."

There he went again with that pompous talk. He only used it when he was about to drop a bombshell. And boy, this time it was a doozy!

"There is no easy way to say this, so I'll launch straight in." He cracked his knuckles and took a good swallow of coffee.

"We are not your birth parents. We…..."

"WHAATT!"

This was not death….it was far worse. I made to stand up and fly to my room.

"Sit down this instant and don't move until I give you permission," ordered my father. "This goes for you too, Cathy. I'm not saying this again so you will listen."

My mother looked completely cowed. It wasn't a bundle of laughs for me either.

"When we were just married, we learned that for physical reasons," - he coughed - "we could no longer have children of our own. Your mother became quite ill and spent some time in a psychiatric unit with her nerves shot to pieces."

Mom put her elbows on the table and rested her face on her cupped hands.

"I knew I'd to do something or neither our marriage nor possibly even your mother, would survive.

"There are still things Christie, I can't tell you because they are not my stories to tell

"Through a contact, I learned of a baby who had been spurned by its father, and the mother, unable to cope, wanted the baby privately adopted so he could never find her again. You will understand that a formal adoption leaves a paper trail."

My blood pressure was returning to normal, and I found myself listening intently.

"Who am I then?" There was dismay in the question but also curiosity.

That I couldn't be theirs was apparent from my straight, raven-black hair and my mother's blonde curls. Strange that I'd always pushed it to the back of my mind.

"You are Anna Christina Heywood, beautiful and accomplished daughter of Julius and Catherine Heywood. That you have always been, and such you will remain until you choose otherwise."

"Well, what do I call you then? Julius and Cathy?" That felt awful.

"There is no reason why your way of life should alter at all Christie. But I want you to know that every decision will be yours to make. We reserve the right to offer advice from time to time but the final decision will be yours alone."

Mom and Dad it was then.

When I needed certainty most I was getting freedom. The two didn't go hand in hand.

"Do I know them…my real…I mean, birth parents?" Mom was silently weeping.

"No, you don't," - well that was a relief anyway - "and I would suggest that for now you leave it that way."

In an almost trance-like state my mother added:

"You were such a beautiful baby. Like Snow White, black hair, satin skin with rosy cheeks. I loved you the moment I saw you. I couldn't have loved a child of my body more. I couldn't ever have let you go, so we did whatever was asked of us. One of those things was not to enquire about your parents and we never have. But I think I know who your mother is, because you are her image when she was younger."

"Well, who is it then?"

"Your mother explained why we can't tell you." said Dad. "The reason still holds. We don't want to lose you baby. Ever."

I was disgusted they'd even contemplate such a thing.

"But you are my parents. You nursed me when I was sick, you wiped my bottom as a baby, you corrected me when I was wrong. How could strangers ever be my parents?"

"But we are so dull," said Julius. "What if your real parents aren't. What if we don't measure up? It's a dread we've lived with for eighteen years."

"Who could have given me more than you have?"

We ended up in a group hug, all three of us in tears. This was a recurrent thing in my life. I made everybody cry – even me.

"I think you should go with your plans. Grace thinks it's okay and we trust her judgement," said Dad, holding Mom firmly in her seat with his hand on her shoulder.

After this horrendous revelation, thank goodness there was the distraction of the move back to Champaign.

That cheered everyone up – it took me precisely zero

days to resettle.

Mom was flitting wound the house with a feather duster and adjusting her prized china figurines on top of newly polished furniture.

But it would be some time until we all came to terms with the situation and meantime we were all trying so hard to be happy it was painful.

As soon as it was politely possible, I called Grace and asked if it was okay if I stayed for a few days later in the month. Of course it was.

She asked if my arm had been amputated yet. Never one to miss a trick, Grace. I never seemed to be able to get my own back.

As there was no band now, Dad gave me an allowance until I could sort myself out. I was still determined to fight my way into the music business but nobody took me seriously, of course. They thought I'd be a music teacher or a designer of some sort. Anyway, something I'd have to go to college for.

I couldn't spin this out forever so I asked Dad if it would be okay to take a year out and to my surprise, he thought it was a good idea. I think I could have asked for anything after the bombshell he'd dropped.

I drove to Windham in my own car. I was so proud. Grace greeted me as I drew up on the gravel drive.

"My God, what's that awful thing you're sitting in. It has to be the ugliest machine on four wheels."

I was nettled. This was my pride and joy. I'd stenciled 'Angel' in flowing script on the trunk and surrounded it with large white and yellow daisies. It was a work of art.

"Never mind, I'll buy you something better for your twenty-first. That'll have to do for now"

I got out of the car. I didn't kiss her.

Later that evening, over a glass of her favorite red wine, I broached the subject of my adoption and what Dad had said.

She wasn't pleased, that much was apparent. But she understood, like my Dad, I was eighteen now and the subject must be broached at some point.

So it turned out I wasn't the person I'd always thought I was. Who was I then? Why hadn't they told me I was adopted from the very start? That was the usual procedure, wasn't it? There must be something else which was part of Dad's 'not my story to tell' routine.

The following day we lazed about in the garden. Grace had donned a wide brimmed hat and elbow-length leather gloves and was pruning a highly scented China rose which was festooned over a trellis. She gave me a wicker basket and told me to cut some of the half-open buds for the hall table.

"Near the gate, there are some budding larkspur. There's a variety of colors. Cut half a dozen stems of the shades you think would match these roses best. They'll add some height."

I wandered down to the gate, breathing in the smell of a rose here, a lily there. A wide blue sky with a few fluffy clouds stretched above, and I spun round seeing the whole as if for the first time, my accumulating mountain of worries shoved into the background if only temporarily.

The house was old enough to have grown moss on the gate posts and the larkspur was flowering next to one of them. So beautiful.

I climbed the brick wall and sat looking at the garden, the lake in the distance and a copse of hackberry trees across a small lane. The air was clean and fresh after the fumes of the city. My life had held few moments of such peace.

A soft breeze off the lake ruffled the leaves on the trees and for a split second, I thought I saw a sweet little face with white teeth and sparkling eyes smiling at me through the branches. Just an illusion because it had gone in a flash.

Nonetheless, I swung my legs over the wall and jumped down on the other side. There was a faint trace of a path between the trees which I followed, jogging. It was good to have my blood pumping again.

On the other side of the copse was a broad alley between two house gardens, leading onto a main road. I picked up pace and looked up the road. A dark blue foreign model open-top was disappearing round a bend in the road. Sitting inside I could just make out the driver, a tiny person because her head was only just visible over the seat-back, and a taller figure, a man with shining blonde hair.

Nah, couldn't be. Just a coincidence. I'd last seen

Harry thousands of miles away in Texas and my lady five years ago. Just a coincidence. And anyway, how could they possibly know each other?

But I was spooked enough not to mention it to Grace.

Chapter Twelve
Rock Star Revealed

I called Jenny to come round the following day. Grace, who loathed pizza, had again provided the largest one ever in the history of the world, and put it in the treehouse.

We both laughed when we saw it. There was no chance in hell we'd get our butts in there now. We spread an old plaid blanket on the ground and sat on it to eat.

I loved Jenny. She was as cuddly as a teddy bear and had freckles across her nose. Her laugh would have done a donkey proud. But she was kind and good natured and had always kept my secrets.

We spent an afternoon dragging out of my bedroom cupboards all the things which make up a little girl's life. All the popstar faces cut from magazines and pasted into tatty old books. Plastic barrettes with bent clips which would no longer fasten. Girlie comic books with pictures of Barbie with pencil holes stuck through her eyes – we didn't like Barbie. And so much more.

Jenny wanted to throw some things away, but I wouldn't hear of it. We packed it all up carefully again and put it back in the cupboards.

The following morning, Grace handed me an envelope with two tickets inside. They were auditorium tickets for a concert by a band called 'Flyte' in the city. Bit of a 'has been' band, once a huge international outfit now they played national gigs only. They seemed to be

doing okay though. Still, it was a free night out and we might enjoy jigging up and down a bit to some oldies. Jenny would love it. She was far more into the nostalgia kick than I was.

There was a whole stream of people going into the theatre. Perhaps I should revise my opinion of their 'has been' status. Seems they still 'were'.

The audience was mostly people my mom's age so it felt a bit odd. A bit like being taken on a carousel by your parents.

Jen had bought a brochure so while we were waiting for the show to begin, I propped myself against a pillar and leafed through it. It was full of colored photos of 'Flyte' through the decades. They were a moderately good-looking bunch. Then I nearly hit the roof.

"It's HIM!" I yelled. "Look…!" I wafted the program under Jenny's nose.

"Who? Who is it?" retorted Jen, overawed by my hysterics.

"It's Harry. Harry Forster."

"Yes, you're right. Is he any good?"

"How would I know?" I brushed the question aside impatiently. "I even saw him yesterday afternoon near Grace's. Why is he following me, Jen?"

Jenny started laughing.

"What're you on, Christie? Why would Harry Forster be stalking you? It's not as if you play piano that good."

At that point, the lights went out, there was a massive drum-roll and three spots lit each band member in succession. Harry was center front. Right in front of me. I prayed to God the footlights were bright enough to hide me.

Jen was jumping up and down like a maniac. I surreptitiously took a few steps backwards. Then, from a safe distance, gave Harry the once-over.

I have to say he was pretty beautiful. Beautiful was the right word. Tall and slender, silken-haired, rimmed spectacles. And over forty, which wasn't so good. And there, hanging loose from his neck, the pendant which was causing all the trouble.

They played a lot of songs. The keyboard player was great. I spent almost the entire first half listening to him.

There was a short intermission.

"Meet you out front later. Enjoy the rest of the show. Gotta find out what's going on."

I pushed my way out of the crowd into the lobby through shouts of "Hey babe. You're goin' the wrong way." No shit.

After walking round for a while, I finally found the stage door and rapped loudly. An elderly man with long sideburns and a cigarette dangling from his lips opened it.

"They'll be signing autographs at a 'meet and greet'

later, if you've bought a ticket."

He made to close the door. I stuck my foot in it.

"I need to see Harry Forster. It's important."

"Yeah. Important for a few hundred other people too."

"No." I said, exasperated. "If you can't let me in, tell him its Christie. He'll want to know I'm here." He will?

"Wait." He shut the door again, ash dropping down the front of his shirt, and I heard the lock turn. I rolled my eyes. I guessed he was used to teenagers slipping past to attack his charges.

Just when I thought he'd not bothered to pass on my message, the door opened on Harry Forster.

I saw a momentary spark of recognition and then his expression became blank, as if he'd never seen me before.

"You want an autograph?" he said in a voice with the slightest trace of a British accent. "Got an album, a brochure or something?"

"Harry, its Christie. You should know me. You've been following me around for years. You helped me in Austin when I was knocked over and hurt my arm. Remember?"

A sign of recognition. Thank God.

"Yeah. I remember now. Did they find the guy?"

What!

"No, they freakin' didn't!"

"Well, if you've nothing to autograph and I don't know you, gotta get back. Show to do."

In desperation I seized the pendant from inside my sweatshirt and dangled it in his face.

"There! Recognize that?"

"Sure do. Where did you get it? You're too young to be initiated."

Initiated? What? No.

"My Aunt gave it to me – Connie Maxwell. Surely you know her. You stood and held her while my aunt drove her car the wrong way up a one-way street. You handed me into the car, dammit!"

It was a measure of my desperation that my language was rapidly deteriorating.

"Connie Maxwell. Nope, can truthfully say I don't know the lady."

So saying, he turned, shut the door and left me gaping, open-mouthed, in the alley.

Oh, shit shit shit! I'd blown what was probably my best chance.

I banged on the door with my clenched fist but there was no response this time.

For want of anything else to do until Jenny came out, I bought a brochure and sat reading it. Even in the pictures he was wearing that damn circle. It was infuriating. I rolled the magazine up and banged it against my leg in frustration. I bought a coke. Something else to do. I was drinking it and staring into space when someone sat beside me. I automatically moved over to give them more room. Someone tapped my arm.

"Please forgive me for asking if I'm wrong, but haven't we met?"

I turned to look into the face of....my lady from the Arboretum. No, it couldn't be! I must have looked like a goldfish. Open-mouthed and totally speechless.

"Oh. I'm sorry. I must have been mistaken. Do forgive me."

She got up to leave.

No, not again…. not this time. I gulped in a lung-full of air and grabbed her arm.

"We…we met years ago. In Champaign. At least I think we did. I was drawing in the Arboretum, and you criticized my work."

"How rude of me" she smiled, sparkly eyed.

"No. You were right. I altered it after you left."

I glanced at her wrist for the diamond bracelet I remembered so well. It wasn't there. Instead, she was wearing a gold charm bracelet which jingled as she spoke. It jingled a lot. I bet if she sat on her hands, she'd be dumb.

I waited for her to say my name which she used last time even though I hadn't told her what it was. But she didn't.

"I'm surprised you recognized me. I was only thirteen or fourteen when we met. I'm eighteen now with make-up and all."

"Oh, I don't know." She studied my face. "Perhaps

it's the nose. You have a very beautiful nose."

Really? Eyes, hair, mouth but she went for the 'nose'?

"Well, it was very nice seeing you again, Christie."

As she disappeared out of the door and into the night, I realized she'd just used my name again. Was she leaving me clues? If she was, she'd struck out.

She knew more about me than I knew about her. We'd discussed my nose, of all things, and my makeup but I hadn't asked her name. Hell'd freeze over before I got round to asking for her number. STUPID!

Two missed opportunities in one evening. Freakin' marvelous! No wonder my Dad thought I was a dead duck as far as further education was concerned.

I took Jen for a burger afterwards and told her about my encounters. She didn't believe me. After a few seconds she saw I was deadly serious and sat down with a bump on her plastic chair.

"Jeez, Christie. You don't mess around, do you? A world-famous rock star and a mystery woman decked in gold and diamonds. "

"Much good it does me when I don't even have the gumption, second time round, to ask her name. And Harry Forster blanked me completely. Or at least I think he did."

"Think? You mean you don't know?"

"Yeah. I think he did. But there was a split second when I could swear he recognized me. Just a glance so I could have been wrong. Then later, he said he remembered helping me when I hurt my arm. But it was that first spark which was interesting."

"Oh, I'm sure you're right," said dear, loyal Jenny. "But there's nothing to do now but keep our eyes peeled and wait for the next time."

"That'll be good. They've already proved they can pop up anywhere in the Continental United States." I said gloomily. Jenny played her ace:

"Let's ask Grace."

Chapter Thirteen

Mysterious Movement

Jenny thanked Grace for the concert tickets then in her forthright manner, went on to tell Grace what had happened, which opened up a whole new can of worms. I'd never even hinted to Grace that I thought I was being followed. Oh boy, was I going to hear about that.

If I hadn't seen her response with my own eyes, I never would have believed it. Grace went chalk-white, and her mouth shut like a steel trap.

"I'll kill the bastard…I'll kill him."

I was longing to yell "Who?" but didn't dare. She was terrifying.

Then she stormed out of the room, slamming the book she'd been reading on the floor with such force the spine broke, and the pages fell out.

What the hell was going on? And who's 'him'?

I drove home the following day. Grace was very terse and hardly looked at me as I left.

I knew I hadn't confided in her about being followed but I didn't think it was that big a deal.

She wasn't happy about Dad telling me about the adoption. Discussing that with her had really made me nervous on the drive over. Although she wasn't exactly happy about the situation, she was at least balanced.

So why would she lose it because someone had been following me? If they'd wanted to rape or murder me, they wouldn't have taken seven years about it. And they wouldn't have sent a cute little pixie with a diamond bracelet or Sir Lancelot either. Although said pixie was well into her thirties and Lancelot had been ditched by Guinevere years back.

Then, to complicate matters further, once I was home again Harry appeared to have been replaced by Bobby, who arrived a couple of days later with…wait for it… Deedee in tow.

My head was beginning to spin.

To say I was gob-smacked was an understatement. Seems Deedee and he'd hooked up in LA where she'd been having training in a vocal school in Tarzana. Her Dad was lecturing somewhere in LA so, as it didn't look as if she was interested in anything else, he financed a singing course. She'd now added jazz to her repertoire and was working the clubs in LA. Bobby smiled at her affectionately. Even though he was twice her age.

"Not sure about the clubs. I was thinking of taking her on tour with the band. But I suppose it's a good way to learn her craft."

Another reason I was surprised was that I was beginning to think Bobby was border-line gay, and Deedee was overtly heterosexual. Guys fawned all over her. Perhaps it was a case of opposites attract.

"Which band are you with?" At last, some kind of coherent question.

"Oh, I'm just a sideman. No-one important."

Another side-step. Deedee hugged me.

"Oh, I'm so pleased Bobby brought me to see you. I really missed you."

Dumb as usual, it didn't occur to me to ask what the heck they were doing in southern Illinois.

"As I recall you left without a word. Some friend!"

"Don't be like that!" she purred. "Pops up and moved us before my mother interfered. They're divorced and have been fighting over me for fifteen years so it's no big deal. But it means I tend to get yanked here and there at a moment's notice."

"I take it you can read and write…. or own a telephone?"

"You're right. But LA is so happening!"

Oh my god, she'd turned into a hippie.

"And once I'd gotten into the music scene, it was impossible to break off. I only have music friends in Los Angeles."

Well, what a nerve! No point in going further down that road or I wouldn't be responsible for my actions.

Fortunately, Bobby intervened, twirling that goddamned pendant round his finger.

"Wouldn't you like to hear her sing? I think you'll be surprised."

I waved them to my piano. He wasn't kidding.

She'd definitely gone old school – Ella Fitzgerald, Peggy Lee and the like. It was great…off the scale.

Bobby was hard-pressed, on the piano, to keep up to the fluctuations and magical vibrato of her voice. Her whole body was consumed by the music and her face transformed.

When the song ended, it took her a second or two to collect herself.

"What do you think?" and she looked as if she really wanted to know.

"I think you should go back to LA but aim higher than a few dingy clubs. Haven't you made any contacts? Apart from Sideman Bobby, that is."

I scowled at him.

"Don't mock" she said. "Bobby knows people. It'll happen."

I applauded her confidence. What she wanted from him was clear to everyone but Bobby it seemed. Better not to burst his bubble.

I turned to her boyfriend and completely changing the subject asked:

"So, Bobby. What about this church of yours?" I swung my pendant round my finger.

"So far, I have one of these from my aunt, Connie Maxwell who nobody seems to know. Harry Forster of 'Flyte', who doesn't know who the hell I am despite having lifted me into a car after a pretty bad assault, has one."

Nothing like milking it for all it was worth.

"And you. What's it about? I might want to join."

Clearly, I was being ironic.

Deedee didn't know what the hell we were talking about but that didn't stop her.

"Yeah, me too. What's it about Bobby?"

Out-numbered, Bobby quailed.

"Well," I said, raising an eyebrow. "Is it a secret like the Hellfire Club? Cloak and dagger? With a philosophy of dark deeds and practices…. human sacrifice or dancing naked in circles?"

"Don't be stupid," said Deedee, rightly. "That's not Bobby's scene at all. He likes 'Flyte' and 'The California Crystal Band' and, you know and ….." she seemed stuck for words and looked at Bobby sheepishly. "and old guys."

I couldn't hide a grin but I needed to keep the pressure on Bobby. Of the three of them, he now seemed the most likely to crack.

"Who're 'The California Crystal Band'?" I asked

"Oh, more old guys" said Deedee dismissively.

"You're getting away from the point again. What's the name of this cult?"

"It's not a cult. It's a 'movement'."

"What's the difference?"

Now we were getting somewhere.

"A cult's controlling and wicked – example, Charles Manson - and a movement is to spread light to the world. Ours is to teach the right way through example. For our own good and the good of everyone we meet."

"Sounds very laudable." I said cynically. "Does it

teach people to stalk other people and frighten then half to death, by popping up round every corner with a weird symbol round their necks? Every single person I meet now I check out for that damn pendant. Its infuriating. If someone's doing good by example here, they're doing a lousy job."

"We are who we are," he replied simply and somewhat incoherently. "Now Deedee. We've seen our friend. Time to go."

"Oh Christie-Crisco" – wow! That was a new one - "Please come to LA and stay in my little apartment by Venice Beach."

Venice Beach? If I went to California I'd be staying in Grace's posh estate in San Clemente, not hanging in a bar with some elderly surfers. Or at least I hoped I would.

Anyway, my conversation with Bobby was a start. But polite as he was, there was a limit to his patience and clearly he was sick of being pigeon-holed by a hippie and an amateur sleuth.

But as I said goodbye on the doorstep, I couldn't completely quash the thought that if I got hold of that little pixie, next time I'd pin her to the ground and sit on her until she came clean.

Chapter Fourteen
World War Three

The situation with Grace was constantly in the back of my mind. Despite an over-riding curiosity to know about that necklace, I had to put things right with her first. She was more like a grandmother than aunt to me, and I hated any bad feeling between us. Even when I couldn't understand what I'd done.

I explained it to my parents as best I could, without giving too much detail. I jumped in 'Angel' and sped off to Windham. I thought it was wise not to tell Grace I was coming. If she was still mad at me she might 'arrange' not to be there.

When I pulled up in the car, I could hear one almighty row going on through the open sitting-room window. To my utter amazement it was between Grace and Connie.

I peeped in surreptitiously. They were standing near enough nose to nose, yelling. You could feel the air almost crackling. I'd never heard either of them swear before, so I was stunned by how good they both were at it.

"What the fuck were you thinking, Connie. You told that bastard where she was and what the hell, you continued to tell him where she was! You'll marry that piece of crap over my dead body."

"How in the hell was I to know he'd report to freakin'

Giulia every word I said! And as for the rest, I'm already Connie Maxwell by name – we've lived together for decades. Everyone knows me as Connie Maxwell – you think your son would tolerate anything else?"

"I told you over and over he was a bastard, and you still didn't believe me. Are you dense, or did you just think I was shittin' you?"

Wow! That was an eye-opener coming from Grace. I'd never see her the same way again.

"For the love of God, Grace, how was I to know he was capable of this amount of hatred? Towards Christie as well as her father."

My father? What did Dad have to do with this? Adoptions apart, he was the most easy-going person I knew. Who could hate him?

It wasn't right of me to eavesdrop, even if I wanted to know more – much more - about what was going on; I'd have to go in. No doubt they'd tell me everything anyway. I banged loudly on the door. A face, Connie's, looked out of the window and when she saw my car, making no effort to lower her voice said:

"Oh shit, Grace. It's her. It's Christie!"

"What the fuck is she doing here! She only went home the other day. Why's she come back?"

"What did you say to her, you old battle-axe?"

Surely I wasn't hearing correctly. Connie turned back into the room and the argument continued.

Before I could learn more, a terrified looking servant opened the door and in a whisper invited me in.

Trembling, she mouthed:

"You might want to wait in the conservatory for a while, Miss."

No frickin' way was I'm missing this. No way. I barged past her and flung the sitting-room door wide.

"So what the hell is going on here? I could hear you at the end of the drive."

They looked at each other. Connie, who was red in the face said:

"I'm so sorry you had to hear us behaving so badly. Did you hear what we were discussing?" *Discussing?*

"Darn right I did. Who hates my Dad? Nobody could hate my Dad. He's not…. hateable!"

I heard Grace heave a sigh of relief. What had I missed? It was clearly something vital.

Making a visible effort to moderate her tone – not an easy thing for her – she said:

"Oh, it's nothing, dear. We were just angry at your Dad for not telling us you were being followed. I'll need to speak to him seriously when I see him."

"Oh no you don't! You scare him to death as it is. And who's Giulia?"

They looked at each other. Neither could come up with an answer quick enough. Connie looked at Grace and shrugged.

"Your birth father belongs to a church. They are keeping tabs on you. I doubt he knows. He wouldn't do anything like this."

Grace had her face in her hands, shaking her head side to side. When she looked up, she was in tears. My whole world shattered. Grace was my rock. I always relied on her to be strong – a port in a storm. But here she was, human. Surprisingly, I loved her for it.

"Well, if he wouldn't – who would?"

"Giulia is his wife," said Grace, "You heard that bit."

"Is she my mother?" I asked aghast.

"No," said Grace, "And that isn't information you'll get from either of us, so don't ask."

Ah, but she'd inadvertently told me Daddy Dearest had been married twice. Once to my birth mother and once to this Giulia woman.

I was otherwise foiled at every turn. It'd take a megaton bomb to shift anything more out of her. I was mentally concocting a list of people who owed me an explanation and Grace was at the top of it.

While it was still in my mind, I ran and took my note pad and ball-point from the glove box of my car. And my overnight bag from the rear seat. If I wasn't staying before, I sure as hell was now!

"I'm going to take a shower." I yelled from halfway up the stairs. I didn't wait for a response.

Once in my room, I threw the pad on the bed and leafed through what I'd got so far.

Bobby: Played keyboards in a backing band. Need to know the name of said band. Member of a strange 'movement' he avoids telling me the name of and wears its emblem round his neck permanently. Hooked up with my erstwhile friend Deedee. Lives in Los Angeles.

Giulia: Pixie lady. No pendant. Birth father's wife. Seems nice. Know nothing else at all.

Grace: knows everything about everything but will tell me nothing not dragged out of her with a billhook.

Connie: apparently Grace's sidekick. Known her all my life. Pretty and continually moist-eyed. Gave me a pendant identical to Bobby's as a special gift, saying it was given to her by someone she loved. How can you know someone well enough to know that her favorite perfume was Chanel and not know where she lives?

Harry: Wears the same pendant as Bobby and me. Major rock-star with a lousy memory. Allegedly. Flits in and out like a butterfly.

Julius and Cathy Heywood, my foster parents who finally told me I was adopted several weeks ago when I was eighteen. Up to that point I hadn't had the faintest idea. Both also know more than they're telling.

And the sum of my knowledge? Practically nothing. I'd thought I'd known everything there was to know about Grace, Connie and my parents but how much of what I thought I knew, was true?

So, back to Bobby. My parents were away in New England on a short vacation, so I invited myself back to Venice Beach to stay with Deedee.

Chapter Fifteen
More Goddam Medallions

I hopped a flight to LA from Chicago. After hiring a car at the airport, I looked for Venice Beach on a map and ended up in a sort of flea market - a tidy, organized flea market, but a flea market nonetheless. Row upon row of neatly folded t-shirts, kaftans and beach towels were displayed, for the mostly disinterested, in tent-like structures which flapped in the hot sea breeze.

The LA beach scene was by this time more skateboard than surfboard. There were bimbettes with bouncy hair and smiles to match, whirling and twirling on their skates between metal poles on the beach front.

The boys weren't what you'd call surfer types. Nothing so fun. They seemed mostly occupied shooting hoops in teams on sand-littered concrete. All very commendable.

Whereas before the boys were once experimental, daring and romantic, they were now clean-cut, wealthy and muscle-bound. And ineffably dull. I couldn't for the life of me figure out where Deedee fit into all this. She was a true sixties chick.

I did eventually find her 'small apartment' and she wasn't kidding. Postage-stamp would have been a better description.

It looked as if it might have been a teenage holiday let

at some point. But she'd cleaned it up, decorated it in bright colors and plush fabrics and scattered mismatched cushions everywhere, which was as well since apart from a fashionably tatty coffee table, there was no other furniture in the room.

The bedroom was wide enough to take a bed which touched the walls at either end, and a small nightstand holding a lamp with a chiffon square draped over the shade, and odds and ends of make-up. Her clothes were hung in a canvas-covered rack in the other corner. There was a shower in the bathroom and a small dinette attached to the living room.

Deedee thought it was 'Just the coolest pad ever'. Truly, I could see her point. It was quaint.

I ended up with the bed because I was the guest, and she took the cushions. She got the better end of the deal.

The following day we took my car through street after street of holiday condos and apartment blocks to Santa Monica and Pico, past the Dodger Stadium which Deedee went into raptures about.

We had to stop so she could photograph the round Capitol building – apparently Mecca. Then on to Universal Studios which I found interesting in a detached sort of way. I liked museums.

I asked to check out central LA which was a mistake. To get there we had to go through a veritable village of small studios and China Town. Deedee pointed out, enraptured, every studio we passed and some up little side-streets we didn't. To me it looked seedy.

The Twinkle in Pa's Eye

We arrived in Central Los Angeles, parked up and Deedee insisted on giving me a guided tour.

It was horrible. People rushing and pushing everywhere, bumping into each other in their haste. Everyone looked distracted and tense – but either very well dressed or…. not. The traffic was appalling, and you truly took your life in your hands on the road, even at pedestrian crossings.

"Isn't it just the best?" enthused my friend. "So exciting, so alive!"

She flicked her strawberry blonde hair over her shoulder and flung her arms in the air like an emoting Marilyn Monroe. In so doing she came close to knocking a small Chinese gentleman through a plate glass window.

Feigned enthusiasm was hard to summon up through my exhaustion. When I was on the point of collapse, she suddenly realized, and we went back to her 'pad' where we showered and rested over coffee.

Then we were off again to her favorite eating spot. I wouldn't call it a restaurant. It was more a cross between MacDonalds and a dive bar. There were booths of stained moquette seating with paper tablecloths. It smelled of beer and the floor was slippery.

Still, the food was great, plentiful and cheap which I supposed was the attraction. The beer wasn't bad either.

"I offered to sing here once but the owner said he couldn't afford to pay me. Which was a shame because at the time I would probably have sung for my supper."

She giggled at her awful joke.

Time to talk turkey,

"So where does Bobby live?"

"Oh, in a mansion in the Hollywood Hills with his parents. I've never been there."

So why would he hook up with a Billie Holliday wannabe from Venice Beach? I'd thought she was using him for contacts but then an awful thought struck me and one I was ashamed of even before I finished having it.

What if he'd been using Deedee to follow me? He did seem to have appeared out of nowhere to give me piano lessons. He'd insisted on playing for Deedee himself. He'd forged a pretty solid link between us. If it was 'church instigated' she must have been in on it. Mustn't she?

Connie had said it was a pretty benign sort of organization so they couldn't have arranged something like this.

Or was she ambitious enough to overlook any ulterior motive Bobby might have in pursuit of her 'career'? That seemed more likely.

So did Bobby know I was here? As he appeared bright and early next day, I suppose he must have. Even so, he did a pretty successful impression of astonishment.

"Hey, Christie," he said, kissing me on the cheek. "Wow, what a great surprise!"

"I thought you were working tonight?" said Deedee

"No. We have just one show left to do in Denver.

Then the band is in the studio for a while, so I'll have time on my hands."

"Contractual obligation, the show?" said Deedee, knowledgeably.

"Yes. We missed a gig because of an electrical fault at the venue. This is by way of a goodwill gesture."

"You'll be out of town then, I guess" said Deedee glumly.

"Yes. Over in Hawaii at my parent's place. A couple of the guys are coming with me. Shame you'll be working."

I thought Deedee was going to cry but she contained it.

"See you when you're back then. Christie'll be here for a day or two to keep me company."

She looked at me for confirmation.

"Until Tuesday, then I have to head back." I said.

Bobby, having determined my future plans, disappeared after hugging us both and kissing Deedee on the forehead. Very passionate. She didn't seem to care.

It wasn't exactly a fascinating couple of days. We wandered up the promenade from Venice to Santa Monica pier. I guess lots of things had changed since the halcyon days of the sixties.

Towards Santa Monica, the sea front was rather shabby, and in places the litter bins were full to overflowing and scraps of paper and paper cups were skittering down the sidewalks.

In the evening, I went with Deedee to the club she was singing at. It was a bit like one of the tiny jazz haunts from the fifties, peopled by beatniks. Her voice was far too big for the room. Her backing band worked as session musicians through the day and were pretty good. One in particular, a percussionist, was excellent.

Deedee sat me at a tiny table to the side of the low platform which served as a stage. It was so dark I could barely see my hand in front of my face until the stage lights came up.

I glanced around at the other customers. It wasn't exactly overflowing. There were groups of three and four scattered around the place.

The most notable people were three guys sitting center front. All three had the obligatory long hair of musicians. All were dressed casually but the portly guy in the center was rather more expensively turned out than the others in tailored shirt and trousers.

As the evening went on, I idly studied the three of them. Two were in their twenties and clearly in awe of the older guy. The young men's body language was bordering on reverential.

When the large gentlemen spoke, they both leaned in as if to catch his every word. They paid rapt attention to the percussionist throughout.

I tried to see the big man's face but all I could make out was a luxuriant beard and a small, well-shaped nose.

When the show finished and the musicians, including

Deedee, had done chatting, they began to pack away their instruments. The three guys moved to a curtain which closed off the back-stage area. They were clearly familiar with the place.

The two young musicians pushed back the drapes and disappeared inside. The big guy went in last and, as he did so, turned to check out the audience and for a split second our eyes met. I don't suppose he even saw me, but I was momentarily overcome by the sadness in his expression. And…..

Oh no, no, no, NO!

He was wearing a fucking pendant like mine. Oh shit. It couldn't be! It was all I could do to stop myself running up and screaming in his face. I came a whisper short of a seizure.

When Deedee came out after getting changed, I grabbed her by the lapels and shook her. "That guy, who's that guy? The one with the expensive shirt?"

"Where?" she said, looking around.

She wasn't being intentionally obtuse but I could have hit her.

"There were three of them sitting together at the front"

"Oh, you mean Gil Robson. He's in here often looking for musicians for his band. He steals the best ones on a regular basis. He's after Jackie, the percussionist, this time. He'll get him too. The whole musical world thinks the sun shines out of his ass. Except the ones he has to work with on a regular basis. He sure drew the short straw with that collection of bastards."

This situation was so exasperating. It was scary but fascinating at the same time.

"Who does he work with then?"

"Not sure. Shiftless set, as far as I can make out. By all accounts Gil is one of the good guys."

"So which band?"

"'The California Crystal Band'. Bobby plays with them sometimes. He's as much in love with Gil as the rest of them. They're so tight it's creepy."

I remembered my Mom talking about them. As a girl, she always fancied Gil's brother, Jamie, who played the drums – the one Phil Taylor tried to emulate. I remember my mother saying she'd been heartbroken when she learned he'd died in a boating accident.

I now had a grand total of four identical pendants. Me via Connie, Bobby, Harry and now Gil Robson. And none of the bastards was giving an inch!

Chapter Sixteen
Return of the Rock Star

Tuesday, as promised, I flew back to Chicago.

Grace picked me up as usual. Her demeanor was still stiff but at least we had a reasonable conversation in the car on the way to Windham.

She told me she was flying to Los Angeles in a couple of weeks to stay at her holiday home in San Clemente. She'd been planning to meet Connie there but she didn't know if they were still speaking. So, everything was up in the air at the moment.

Anyway, would I like to go with her. I thought it over for long enough that she glanced at me curiously. I had an awful feeling that if I went, I would have to act as arbiter between them. I'd no intention of doing that. It would mean I would have to take sides. The thought was too awful to contemplate.

"I know what you're thinking," said Grace - of course she did - "I wouldn't put you in that position and neither would Connie. But I do have to confess to an ulterior motive. At least if you're there, we'll have to be civil with each other."

And the air will be blue, I thought.

"And Connie could bring my grandson Simeon with her. When he called her Mom I used to wonder if it was 'tongue in cheek', but when you see them together you'll realize that's what she is to him. I won't have either of the other two anywhere near me."

It always shocked me that she should refer to her own son like this, but she was the most rational person I knew so I supposed she must have very good reasons.

She finally talked me round, as we both knew she would, and I agreed to go with her on the proviso it was okay with Mom and Dad.

I knew there would be no problem. Dad was always distracted by work and a bit late in life, Mom had become something of a social butterfly. Largely to do with her new-found fascination with Bridge.

So I'd lots of time to batter the piano into submission. I hadn't played in a while and hadn't realized how much I'd missed it. It wasn't the same without Deedee's voice, but I added my appalling vocals and it got me by.

I spent a bit of time trying to draw some of the older University buildings, but soon discovered I was better at fluid than straight lines, so I went back to the Arboretum. After six, admittedly sporadic, years I was beginning to find it a bit tedious, so I looked about for other inspiration.

I found it in figure drawing. I liked that a few quick lines for direction meant I could go home and finish in relative comfort. When that failed to be enough, I took my pocket camera with me and did a bit of surreptitious snapping.

I even saw Harry frickin' Forster once, walking across one of the college lawns. But he was too far away and facing away from me. He was so ubiquitous I was starting to think he'd another connection to the

University: perhaps a friend or brother there or the girl on his arm in the restaurant. Although I'd never seen her before or since, that didn't mean anything. Students came and went all the time although not often from Texas to Illinois.

My parents returned from their trip that weekend. They had had a lovely time and looked fit and healthy from all the walking. I'd missed them, much to my surprise. Funny, when someone's there all the time you tend not to notice them.

I asked them about going to San Clemente with Grace, and my mother's expression suddenly altered. She pulled herself together quickly and became unnaturally cheery.

It immediately put me in mind of another incident which I should have forgotten. It was surprising that I remembered it because it occurred before we went to Austin over four years ago.

"Before we moved, I heard you and Dad talking in the kitchen. You didn't know I was there."

It was as if they both knew what was coming. I could see their brains whirring trying to think up any answer quickly enough. Seemed to be a common problem for the adults in my life.

"Did you know I was being followed and have been since I was first in my teens?" They began to speak at once, but I held up my hand to stop them.

"Don't even bother! Why would you want to take me to Austin to hide me from someone? Apart from you, I'm only being stalked by a pixie, a major pop star -

possibly two, and a backing band member – you know him, Bobby. Also, possibly the lead singer of my own band. I'm getting more than a bit pissed off!."

I yelled the last sentence and waited for the fall out. I'd never sworn at my parents before but at that moment I couldn't give a shit.

"I've told you. You know all I'm at liberty to say. Why do you keep on about it?," insisted my Dad.

It was then that, for the first time in my life, I truly lost it. I couldn't speak for rage so I left, slamming the door behind me.

I'd no idea where I was going or what I was doing. My head was buzzing, my heart was pumping. I began to run and run until I could go no further. The physical exercise calmed me and left me exhausted.

I sank down on the grass with my back against a tree and burst into tears.

Everyone I knew and loved seemed bent on making my life a misery. They must have a reason. I could be awkward and self-willed but I wasn't bad enough for even strangers to hate me.

I sensed, rather than felt, a presence behind me and suddenly was dragged into a comforting hug.

"What the hell….." That was as far as I got. I stopped, stunned.

"Harry Forster? What in God's name are you doing here?" I said, and as an afterthought, "And what, for chrissake, are you doing. Get off!"

I pushed away the guy most of the female half of the western world would have been doing the opposite to.

"Last time I saw you, you didn't even know who I was…. you bastard!"

Most of my temper had dissipated but not all.

He held out his hand but let it drop before it reached my arm. He looked troubled and emotional. He'd a nervous way of pushing his glasses up on his nose, I noticed.

"I want you to know I'm not okay with this," he said.

"What?" I was getting better.

"This keeping a check on you. Everyone has a right to freedom – except you it would seem."

It was a relief that someone else seemed to understand this. And it was a comfort to know I wasn't out of my mind.

"Why?" Let him do the talking. His distress increased and he looked at me earnestly.

"Please, please believe me, I would tell you if I could. It breaks my heart that I can't. But I have a responsibility to someone I love dearly and can't betray"

"Betray?" Loquacious.

"Please, may I?" and he pulled me to his chest and rested his chin on my head. If this is what it was like when he was strumming his guitar on Haight Ashbury, I could go with that. I felt warm and comforted and for a few moments, all my fears melted away."

"Please don't be angry. All that has happened has been done with love. For you as well as others. In the fullness of time, I promise you faithfully you will know everything. The time isn't right just yet."

I didn't know him but somehow he drew me in.

"If you understood what it was like to be trailed every day of your life you wouldn't do this."

"I can see that," he said gently.

"Sometimes I get very scared. I don't know who you are, or even how many you are. Are there people watching me I don't know? Apart from you?

"I was in LA visiting a friend last week. Bobby was there. And I saw a man in a club who also wore the pendant. Was he following me too?"

"Describe him for me."

"Oh, I know his name. I just wondered if he was one of the people tailing me. He's the singer from 'The California Crystal Band', Gil Robson. He was in the club my friend was singing at checking out their percussionist."

"Rest assured, Gil is definitely not one of us."

His smile turned into a chuckle but he didn't elaborate.

"I have to go. Please understand you are loved and cared for. Perhaps we may speak again soon."

He got up and melted away into the shadows like a ghost.

Chapter Seventeen
San Clemente

I did decide to go to San Clemente. It would help Grace out if she needed it which I doubted, but it would also give me space to get over the spat with my parents.

My Dad tried to apologize but as by now I was questioning his sincerity, I thought the break might do us both good.

And as for my Mom, it appeared to me she and Connie were as bad as each other. Would Connie give me a clue? Highly doubtful on past experience. Perhaps they were just so different. My mom was a true domesticated housewife from Illinois. Connie was a sophisticated lady from California.

The last reason for my decision was Harry. His distress had really shaken me, and it was good to know I had an ally, albeit reluctant, in the other camp. It was a relief to know the entire Movement hadn't ganged up on me - only a few of them. That must make the problem easier to solve. What did they all have in common? It would seem Gil Robson was not involved. Not everyone with the emblem was following me or necessarily knew of my existence.

Grace and I arrived in San Clemente and I was relieved she'd returned to her normal self.

We were picked up at the airport by her gardener – she thought chauffeurs an unnecessary expense.

Grace's summer residence was situated high on a

cliff, unusual in Southern California, and was reached by a narrow metaled road, lined with her favorite rhododendrons, which zig-zagged up the hillside. On the wall next to the door was a slate plaque with Ginsling House written in script.

Ginsling House itself was actually built into the cliff and commanded a stunning view of the town of San Clemente with its promenade and famous pier. Beyond was an endless stretch of turquoise ocean fading into a pale horizon.

The front comprised a glass wall with a sliding door and a terrace the size of a large living room, with all the paraphernalia for outdoor enjoyment: a wrought-iron Italian-tiled dining suite, three easy chairs and a sofa with overhanging shades, a large barbeque, various coolers and a small freezer for ice and ice cream. Very impressive and a bit frightening.

It became less so when Grace flung aside the door, threw her purse and jacket across one of the chairs and yelled in a voice which could shatter glass:

"Tina, where the hell are you?"

A flustered little Mexican lady in a black dress hurried through the door, trying desperately to tie a starched white apron round her waist.

"Si, Senora?"

"English, Tina…English!"

Having frightened the poor woman half to death she said in a soft voice:

"Lemonade please. Get Mary to prepare a light lunch. No rush."

Tina hurried off.

Grace grinned. She could be evil that way.

She flopped into a chair with a sigh of relief and kicked off her shoes.

"We'll eat then I'll give Connie a call. See if she's still speaking to me."

That proved unnecessary. Connie had rung Windham to apologize but was told by Grace's staff she'd already left for San Clemente.

Later that afternoon she arrived at the villa, driven by Simeon Maxwell. The way Grace had spoken of him, I expected him to be a boy, but he turned out to be a pretty gorgeous twenty-five-year-old with a deep, natural tan, sapphire blue eyes and a smile to melt granite.

Connie introduced him as Simm and I'm ashamed to say I blushed when he kissed my cheek. He smelled gorgeous too – lemon grass and musk. Connie chuckled and gave me a hug.

"I knew you two would get along," she said, although how the hell she knew that I couldn't imagine.

Meanwhile, Simm had picked Grace up in both arms and was swinging her round like a carousel.

"And how's Grannie?" he asked, as he put her down again. She'd to lean against him for a moment or two until she stopped being dizzy.

"You son of a bitch! You do that again and I'll cut you out of my Will!"

But it was easy to see this was a standing joke between them. They hugged warmly.

He went back to Connie and draped his arm casually around her shoulders.

"You taking me for a fish supper, Momma?"

"I have a better idea. Why don't you take Christie, buy her supper and show her around the town? Better than sitting here with two old ladies!"

"Mature, not old," admonished Grace.

Thankfully, normality had reasserted itself.

Simm couldn't have been more charming. He bought me lobster thermidor so I could try something I'd never had before. I had a feeling, by the waiter's smirk it was expensive, but Simm didn't seem to mind. He wrapped his sweater round my shoulders when I shivered and even laughed at my jokes.

By the time we returned, Grace and Connie had well and truly buried the hatchet, and not in each other I was pleased to see.

But the lighthearted atmosphere dissipated instantly when Simm asked quite casually, if his father would be spending some time with us over the weekend. I watched him carefully. The question was not perhaps as innocent as it first appeared,

"Goddamn, Simm!" exclaimed Grace. "Why did you have to spoil a perfectly good afternoon?"

"Oh Gran – forgive and forget. He's not that bad."

"Be glad to if every time I forgave he didn't forget to return the favor," said Grace dryly. "And I would ask that while you are here, you would kindly refrain from offering your own invitations. I have very good reason for not wanting him here."

Connie sat stiff-backed throughout this little exchange. She looked strained and I wondered what it was she'd wanted to talk to Grace about so much they had both made sure we were out of the way.

The following morning, while Simm splashed around in the pool, we ladies decided to take in the shops. We visited the Avenida Del Mar which had shops from secondhand books to designer boutiques. I had a great time poking about in bins in a shop which sold boho gear at ridiculous prices.

I lost the other two for a few minutes when I tripped on the corner of a Persian rug and fell awkwardly against a tall long-haired man dressed in an old-fashioned ankle-length kaftan. He righted me and went on looking through a basket of shell beads on the counter, but I saw him watch me leave the shop with a puzzled expression, as if he'd seen me before. Not a clue who he was.

He was quickly forgotten when Connie insisted on buying me the most gorgeously romantic Elana Kattan dress, simply because I said I liked it. I did, honestly, try to dissuade her but perhaps I could have been a little more insistent. But for me, honor was satisfied when I explained I never went anywhere I could wear it, and she said not to worry we'd fit some social life round the dress. Who could say no?

When we got back to Ginsling House, Simm had gone

surfing with some buddies from LA.. Grace and Connie went to their respective rooms to recover from our arduous shopping trip, so I decided I'd go and do a little exploring of my of my own.

Chapter Eighteen

Kidnapped

There was no point in going down the road, it was too steep for comfortable walking, so I moved to the side. Underneath Ginsling House, the terrace was supported by pylons of screed concrete.

The gap beneath followed the slope of the cliff and was open to the elements at the front.

At one time it seemed to have been laid out as a covered play area for children. But since one generation had grown up and the next was not yet born, all the toys and furniture were packed away in plastic boxes and stored against the far wall.

This left an area which contained a vintage Bentley in much need of repair and an old barrel organ covered with a tarpaulin.

I pulled the cover away and examined the organ. It had automata at the front, painted wooden figures in Tudor costume. I pressed one or two of the keys, but the metal was rusted shut by the sea air, and the paint had flaked badly from parts of the wood, leaving it exposed.

I knelt down to see if it was rotten beneath the paint when there was a soft step behind me. A gag was tied tightly round my mouth. A sinewy arm wrapped round my waist and pulled some kind of canvas bag over my head.

For a moment I was so shocked I couldn't react. Then

I fought and kicked and struggled. But the arm only tightened and a quiet voice whispered:

"Keep your mouth shut and stop struggling and you won't get hurt."

Like hell that was going to work! I tried screaming through the gag but could only manage a muffled croak.

He slapped me across the head with his free hand. It hurt. He pushed me to the floor and tied my hands behind my back.

My reaction was opposite to the one he expected. I yelled louder and kicked harder. I was too mad to be scared. This bastard would get all I could give.

I was dragged protesting to a car parked so far as I could tell, behind the first big rhododendron bush on the winding lane to the main road. I was manhandled into the back seat and the door slammed shut.

I tried to wriggle my hands free, but they were tied with rope much too tightly to work loose. My one advantage was that I could just see out of the bottom of the bag over my head. It wasn't much but it gave me a sense at least of direction.

At the bottom of the lane we turned right along the Pacific Highway. I tried to guess at the distance but I couldn't - we seemed to be moving a long time.

After a while, the traffic seemed to increase and the car I was in stopped and started more. I began to hear the sound of voices, children, teenagers laughing. Then the reverse happened and we were back on the open road again.

I began to feel suffocated. The gag was too tight round my head and I couldn't move it. The bag was making me sweat. I couldn't breathe. Desperately, I kicked out at the front passenger seat and made whatever noise I could through the gag.

The car pulled off the road and the traffic noise became an occasional hum. The door opened and someone got hold of me by the scruff of the neck and roughly pulled off the canvas bag and removed the gag.

It took a second or two for my eyes to adjust to the light and then I screamed at the muscle-bound monster in front of me.

"You bastard. What the fuck do you th……."

My shout was cut off by a slap to the face which knocked me to the ground. I rose to my hands and knees, shaking my head to clear it. I was grabbed by the arm and hoisted to my feet then shoved forward, hands still secured behind me.

I glanced covertly around me trying to commit to memory the house and grounds. It wasn't a house so much as an estate.

It comprised three houses, a variety of swimming pools and pool houses, a putting green and some tennis courts. All were set on a series of stepped lawns edged with crazy-paving paths. This was the front and what I could see of the sides of the main house.

The drive on which we walked, seemed endless. That was probably because by this time I was dehydrated and exhausted by panic.

In the house, I was pushed into a room which could only be described as a conservatory. It was attached to the outer wall but the sides and front were formed by trellises holding two enormous grape vines, laden with fruit.

Chapter Nineteen

Cindy and the Meditating Snake

In the center of this conservatory, sitting cross-legged on a small Persian prayer mat, was a very strange figure. He appeared to be asleep sitting up, but as I was shoved in front of him, he opened one eye, took in my appearance then closed it again. I can't have been a pretty sight because he frowned and said in a quiet, lethal voice:

"I said no violence. If you had to damage her, it shouldn't have been the face. Go away. I'll see to you later."

The lacky sloped off like a whipped child.

The silence went on until I could feel my temper rising again. I thought I'd had it knocked out of me but the adrenaline which was keeping me upright was also making me reckless.

"Sit down," he said, still with his eyes closed, indicating a small tapestry-covered stool with carved panels.

"If you'd open your damned eyes a moment, you'd see I can't because my hands are tied behind my back." I growled, and twisted sideways, tapping my foot, so he could see.

"Come here," then more impatiently, "Come here so I can take the rope off."

He picked up a curved knife from a joss stick laden table to his left and cut through my bonds. I shook and rubbed my wrists and arms to get some feeling back.

"Now, sit down," he grated.

While he appraised me, I took the opportunity to check him out too. This son of a bitch was going to pay the price for this!

Could have been the guy I'd bumped into while shopping that morning – sure looked like him. It had only been a brief encounter so I only had a vague recollection of his appearance.

He was wearing a beaded leather band round his forehead. His features were delicate and he had a small scar on his left cheekbone. His nose was small, and slightly hooked, but his mouth was his most telling feature. It was thin-lipped and the lines around suggested he was given to ill-temper.

He was dressed in an old-fashioned Indian cotton kaftan with gold edging. The four buttons at the neck appeared to be large cabochon rubies. His feet, protruding from the kaftan, were bare, but had intricate designs painted on them in henna. He closed his eyes.

"Omm," he said with a slight vibrato.

"What?" I said.

"Omm is the sound of the Universe, ignorant girl."

He glared at me with a stare which made me shudder – his eyes were a cold and piercing pale blue. He leered.

"You are very much to my taste. Long black hair is my very favorite. Reminds me of your mother."

What the hell was he talking about? My Mom was blonde…..but, no, she might very well not be. I'd no idea who my birth mom was. Did I know anyone with straight black hair? Nope. So it wasn't someone I knew.

He got to his feet in one fluid movement which reminded me of a snake.

Grabbing me by the wrist, he dragged me behind him through to the back of the house. There, a large swimming pool was filled with girls in various stages of undress. Most were diving or playing in the pool. Some were laid out on the lawns, eyes shut, sunbathing.

"Cindy, this is Christie?" He looked at me for confirmation. I didn't. "Usual treatment but let her wash first."

He walked back to the house whistling softly.

Cindy who was clearly in charge of the girls, looked okay. She put her arm round my shoulders and gave me a slight squeeze.

"You're going to love it here. Ed's a really good guy. Now come on, you can take a shower and I'll give you a change of clothes. You'll feel much better after that."

The shower renewed my energy, and I set about digging into the sandwiches and cake which a servant placed on a large low table. The other girls came in in ones and twos and ate with us. They seemed happy and content. Perhaps it wasn't going to be as hard as I thought getting out of here.

One of them took out a guitar and began to sing a gentle song, and slowly the others joined in. Their harmonies were exquisite.

"Good, aren't they?" whispered Cindy in my ear.

The music was beguiling and I slowly began to sway to it – it made me feel relaxed and sleepy.

"I told you you would like it here."

The chocolate from the cake tasted delicious, warm and moist on my tongue.

This was all wrong. I shook my head to clear it but I sank back on the rug and ran my hands over its soft pile. I would float away if I let it go.

The next thing I knew, I awoke from a deep sleep, my clothes had been removed and I was laying on my back on the lawn. I sat up, trying to cover my nakedness with my hands and arms.

"Cindy," I yelled over the laughter in the pool. "I need something to wear that's not a bikini or my birthday suit."

She disappeared and came back with the same kind of kaftan her master wore, minus the rubies.

"What happens if I try to escape?" I asked, fearing this would go straight back to Ed.

"I don't know. I assume all those who don't want to stay are free to leave. The only thing I've seen is Ed waving them goodbye. They seemed happy enough so I just assumed he was having them taken home."

Hmm, really?

"What does he do with all these girls? They're like hamsters running round and round and going nowhere."

"I'm here permanently, but the others use this as a

jumping off point for greater things. Almost all of them want to be dancers. Ed can help them with their ambitions."

"How?"

"He uses them on-stage. Of course you've heard of 'The California Crystal Band'? They were very big in the sixties. – he was one of the founder members.

"A few years ago, Ed left – I believe there had been a huge argument and they all stopped talking to each other. He walked out and set up his own outfit, calling them 'Harmony'. Well, 'Harmony' sound the same, but lately are beginning to look their age. Ed thinks these young girls bring some energy to the shows. The high kicks and splits some of these girls can do make your eyes water. Make Ed's light up though."

There was just the trace of suppressed emotion, the tiniest, before she smiled sweetly and lit a joint.

Breathing it in deeply, she passed it to me. I shook my head.

"No thanks. I've just been down that path and didn't like the outcome. I didn't appreciate what was foisted on me earlier either. That wasn't fair."

"I know. But its what's expected. If he wants to take you to bed I suggest you don't object unless you want to see his bad side."

I pointed at my bruised face.

"Bad side? The thug who abducted me did this. Apparently he wasn't supposed to mar 'it'."

"Oh, that's good" said Cindy. "He must be intending to send your picture to someone for ransom. Don't laugh - it's happened before."

"If you don't like it here, why don't you leave?"

"I know too much of what goes on here for him to ever let me go. But for those who aren't leg-kickers, I try to find a way out. How successful I am I don't know, but I never see them again."

Two days later, I was sent for to go up to the house. Cindy took me, her face a mask. What would he do to me?

But he just wanted to take a look at my ruined face to see if I was photogenic enough yet. He grabbed my chin and moved my face around. Clearly, it didn't meet with his approval and he frowned. I didn't like him touching me. I found him repulsive.

After that I was taken to see him daily, until five days later he found my face recovered enough for the camera. He still had to bring in his makeup artist to finish the job.

He must have done this before, as he'd a paid photographer. He seemed a nice guy, so Ed must have had something on him. I doubt he'd have gotten involved in something so shady otherwise.

A couple of days later, when I'd been in captivity for a week, he sent for me again. Ed was sitting behind a highly polished desk in a room with tall bookshelves. A place less like my father's study I couldn't imagine. It was clean to the point of sterility.

He'd a red splodge of paint on his forehead and had his eyes closed, his hands positioned as in prayer.

Such a conflict of extremes! He was trying to be

something he was incapable of. Every word he spoke, every facial expression he made, illustrated he would never achieve the Nirvana he so clearly desired. How sad. It made me smile.

He opened his eyes and slapped his hands down on the desk.

In front of him was a manilla envelope. It had an address typed on it. I tried to read it upside-down but could only make out Colorado.

The envelope wasn't sealed and he drew out an A4 photograph of my face. He turned it over and scrawled on the back in a hand not his own, were the words.

"Hello, Daddy Dearest.

Meet your little girl'.

"How about that? And no word of a lie. Don't you just love it?"

"No I don't. There's only one way that could be true and that's if I had two fathers which I clearly don't. My parents live in Illinois and I can assure your there's only one 'daddy'."

"Keep thinking," he encouraged.

Whatever, I mustn't let slip I knew I was adopted. That would only give him more ammunition against the poor man who was my birth father, so I acted ignorant.

"No. Can't help you. Drawing a complete blank."

"Well, we'll just bait the hook shall we? And see what happens?"

I didn't like his smile one bit.

Cindy checked me over carefully when I went back to the pool. She seemed surprised.

"He didn't touch you? You must be very special. He has something particular planned for you. Most of them" - she stared in the direction of the prancing girls - "have been well and truly bonked in the first couple of days. Some actually liked it."

She sounded cynical with a touch of jealousy. Odd combination.

Chapter Twenty

Enter the Cavalry

―――∘⌒☉∘⌒∘―――

A whole week and no communication from outside. What had happened to the stalkers who had dogged my every step for the past five years? Now they weren't there, I felt bereft - and a bit scared because no-one was looking out for me.

Every time I tried to look over the tall retaining wall, I was warned back by a muscle-bound lacky in sunglasses. There seemed to be quite a few of them. Once, I tried to climb over a perimeter wall and got my leg scraped from thigh to ankle with special emphasis on my knee, by a Terminator look-alike. They must have worked shifts because they were there all night as well. I know because I got caught again. Matching legs – not pretty.

Cindy was at heart a good person, and the rough treatment I was getting didn't sit well with her.

"Do you have something personal, anything, which only those who know you would recognize and is big enough to see from the road?"

I thought it over, but it seemed hopeless. All my clothes had been taken when I arrived. I still had my pendant but it was too small to be of use.

"A phone number and an innocuous message only one person would understand?"

I gave her Grace's San Clemente number and the name 'Anna'. Only Grace and Connie besides my

Mom and Dad, would know it was my first name.

Cindy came by later that afternoon to tell me she'd called the number, given the name and told them to trace the call. Of course it was a listed number but bullying a telephone company employee was Grace's specialty. Nothing would stop her getting to me if she'd even half a clue.

"You're not going to get into trouble if Ed finds out?" I asked.

"Not if I'm not caught. As that's all I'm doing, I don't think that's going to be a problem. Keep away from me for a while though. We mustn't look as if we're in cahoots." Ca -what?

For the first time in days I allowed myself a smile. This idiot was no match for Grace. She'd wipe the floor with him. I sent up a little prayer to please let me be there when she did.

Well it took less than twelve hours which was going some even for Grace. She stormed up the drive with half of Orange County Police Department in tow. The sergeant in charge had a haunted look which public officials often adopted when dealing with my beloved Grace. Connie was there but stayed hidden in the car.

Sometimes God answers prayers. I was present when Grace confronted Ed. Oh joy!

She got hold of him by the hair and swung him round until her fist connected with his nose. For a little refined old lady she could sure pack a punch. The spirit matched his rubies beautifully and went on to decorate the rest of the front of his kaftan. Very tasteful.

A police officer made a move to restrain her and was in his turn, held back by his superior who, afterwards, slipped into the shadows to hide his amusement.

"You abduct my baby and you expect to get away with it, you miserable piece of excrement?"

She picked up the nearest object, which fortunately for him happened to be a cushion. It might just as well have been the knife on his incense table, it wouldn't have made an iota's difference to Grace. She swung it round and hit him over the head hard enough to knock him sideways, then she continued to belabor him until he begged the police for protection. Strangely, none of them seemed to have accompanied Grace into the room.

I was only there because Cindy had grabbed me by the arm and dragged me through the house. Even she seemed to be enjoying the spectacle.

Between blows Ed managed to get out:

"You're making a big mistake lady. I know who she is and if you don't stop I'll broadcast it to the world."

Naturally he'd underestimated Grace. She told Ed's photographer Ed was going to jail and offered him a truck load of cash to take some shots for her instead.

She got hold of Ed by the hair next to his ear – the bit that really hurts – and dragged him through the house where the nymphettes were ducking and diving in the pool, giggling and splashing while a couple of them sat on the edge smoking joints and looking nicely glassy-eyed.

Grace held him there while the photographer walked round the pool, photographing the scantily clad girls, making sure Ed was in the background of every shot.

By this time the whole world seemed to be laughing at Ed Morris - including Cindy.

I enjoyed every minute. It was like being rescued by the cavalry.

"No…mister. Do your worst but if you do, rest assured, these pictures will be on the front page of every tabloid in America."

Nothing he could say, nothing he could do, except cry tears of frustration.

Still holding Cindy by the hand, I walked back out to the car. This was her doing and I wanted her to come with us. When I asked her, she sadly shook her head and said that for better or worse her life was here now.

I kissed her on the cheek and hugged her tightly, then turned and slid into the car next to Connie, who had shrunk almost entirely into the footwell.

"You can get up now" I said, assuming she was there because she was appalled by Grace's behavior.

"No," she whispered, "He knows me. It would be a disaster if he saw me."

When I asked where she knew him from she became very vague.

"Oh, you know. Helping out at concerts and things."

We went back to San Clemente where Grace went to bed. Me too. I was exhausted. Connie sat on the terrace with a large glass of red wine and tears dropping off her chin. We were all in a state of shock for different reasons, but I think it was probably worst for Grace. She was getting on in years and couldn't take that level of stress without repercussions. I could kill the bastard, if only for that.

By the time we were all together again, Connie had spoken to Simeon on the phone. He was in the process of packing as much of his stuff as he could get into his car and then was driving over to us.

Grace had told him some small details of his Dad's misdemeanors. Not much but enough for him to leave in disgust.

Simm would countenance no harm or disrespect to Connie by anyone. His grandmother – amazingly Oliver's mother – had offered him the house until he could get sorted out. Grace would be 'going home for a rest'.

Simm jumped out of his car and dashed into the house. From the look of him I guessed he'd driven much the same way from Los Angeles.

He ignored Connie and I and picked his grandmother up as if she was made of china. He sat her on his knee, brushed her hair back and kissed her forehead.

"Get off" said Grace and got up in a huff, straightening her skirt.

Simm laughed loudly.

We were all feeling much better.

After I'd showered, changed and fixed my face, Simm took us all out for dinner. Halfway through I looked round the table at each in turn and knew how much I loved them. Dearer to me, even, than my own parents.

Chapter Twenty-one

Murder and Other Mayhem

The following day, we waved goodbye to Simm. Connie moved into her mother's old house in Santa Monica and Grace and I flew back to Chicago. I stayed overnight in Windham, picked up Angel and drove home.

My parents were blissfully unaware of my time as a kidnap victim, and I'd asked Grace and Connie to leave it like that. I was keen to get back to normal as soon as possible.

Very soon, I began to see the people I now thought of as my guardians. There was another of them. A pretty cool young guy with long hair and great pecks. He looked familiar, as if he'd always been hovering in the background unnoticed. Well, the more the merrier.

Being a University town, it didn't take me long to get another gig. I couldn't go on sponging off my Dad forever.

Sadly, no Deedee this time. Inept she may have been but she was reliable in her fecklessness. I could work round that.

We had a lead singer of sorts, but he thought he was Jim Morrison and his singing wasn't much better than mine. He'd do until something better came along.

And what was it with drummers? Were they all the same? I never met one who wasn't loud, self-opinionated and with long hair. And the bass player was always the absolute opposite.

I worked hard at my piano skills. My tastes had altered. Because I was growing up I guessed.

Jerry Lee had been replaced by Elton John, Fats Domino by Alan Price - very British stuff. Much more tuneful and laid-back but completely different.

I loved it. That I was widening my repertoire was beside the point - I was having such a good time. Of course this enthusiasm bore fruit. When you get such a kick out of something, you draw others along with you. We started off jamming and ended with some reasonable engagements. Even fronted for some bigger bands.

Although the contretemps with Ed was over, it stuck in the back of my mind and made me jumpy and distracted.

I didn't see my little pixie lady or her cohorts so much. Either they weren't around or they had become better at hiding from me. I suspected the latter.

I did see Harry once or twice though. His girlfriend – the one I'd seen him with in Austin - appeared to have relocated to the Department of Contemporary Music at the University in Champaign. I saw her walk through the door there a couple of times.

I suspected Deedee had bullied Bobby into a trip to Hawaii. Anyway, they weren't around.

I once glimpsed the smiley long-haired guy who seemed to wear t-shirts whatever the weather - tough as well as sexy. He waved at me and slipped round the corner of an electricity sub-station by the Science block. Hmm, must check him out. No medallion but that wasn't necessarily an issue – the lady didn't have one either.

A couple of weeks later, I was eating toast, drinking coffee and reading the latest copy of Rolling Stone the paper boy had dumped on our porch that morning, when the phone rang.

"Hey Grace. You good?"

I guessed not since she was coughing and spluttering at the other end of the line.

"Have you got a copy of the Tribune there?" She was never without the latest edition of the Chicago Tribune. Didn't mean I was, though.

"'Cause not. Why?"

"Go get one and call me back. NOW!" She slammed the phone down. I looked down the receiver in shock. Wow! Had someone dropped a nuclear bomb?

I grabbed my jacket, hopped into my trainers and ran for the nearest convenience store which was two blocks away. I grabbed the last copy of the Tribune from the rack, slapped coins on the counter and opened it out.

"OH MY GOD!"

I ran all the way back home and spread the newspaper on the table. The banner headline ran:

"LEAD SINGER OF BAND 'HARMONY' AR-RESTED FOR MURDER',"

and underneath:

"Girl Found Dead in Cellar of California Mansion"

Beneath, was a picture of Ed struggling in the grasp of two burly police officers as they tried to put him in handcuffs. His face was contorted in horror.

I rang Grace back. I could tell she was pacing with phone in hand.

"Did you read it?" she said testily.

"I rang you back straight away like you said. I've seen the headlines but not the article."

"The girl.... the girl who helped you. It's her. Her name was Cindy, wasn't it? Read it. I'll wait."

I picked up the paper and scanned the article. Then I read it properly in dawning horror.

It didn't say why, but she'd been locked in an old cellar under the main house. There he'd just simply forgotten about her. Within a week she'd died of dehydration and starvation. The police were tipped off by one of his other employees, a security man by the name of Maurice Mercer, who had himself been alerted by a female companion of Mr. Morris – that was Ed - but they were too late.

This was all my fault. I should have made her come with us. I should have trussed her up and shoved her in the car next to Connie. I didn't. I didn't! She'd risked herself to help me get out of there because she knew I was in danger, and this was what had happened. I could never, ever forgive myself.

I might not be able to kill that bastard Morris, but I could see he got his just desserts. I didn't know just how yet but I'd find a way.

Grace rapped her receiver on something hard and said:

"Are you still there or have you dropped off to sleep? Well, what are we going to do? We can't just leave it at that."

"*We* are not going to do anything. *I* am going to see what I can find out from his staff. I want Mr. Morris to stay where he is for a very long time. Did you know he threatened to blackmail my birth father? He said he knew perfectly well who my birth parents are. More than I do." I grumbled.

Grace tutted. I could have killed her. Was my father a mass murderer? Was he Quasimodo? What the hell was wrong with him that no-one so much as mentioned his name? And my mother? I knew she'd long black hair like mine but that's not a lot, is it? I rang Simm and asked if it was okay for me to stop over in San Clemente for a couple of days and flew to Los Angeles.

Chapter Twenty-two
Strange Encounters

I needed information. Perhaps the place to start was Ed's home. I'd have to be careful. I didn't know which of his staff could be trusted. Son of a bitch that he was, I couldn't imagine there were many loyal employees, but apart from helping me, Cindy had been loyal, hadn't she? And just look what happened to her.

I was hoping there were others who had come to the same conclusion. Especially Maurice the Muscle. He and Ed hadn't parted on good terms. He might be a good place to start, although I hadn't exactly been his favorite person either.

I wasn't sure exactly what I was looking for, but Ed was such a toad I was sure there must be plenty of dirt to dish.

I drove past oft-deserted strips of golden sand, past limitless turquoise ocean, through a small seaside holiday town, until I reached my destination.

This time I was pleased to see my guardians, never intrusive, always elusive.

In the open like this the only one to ever acknowledged me was the one I'd christened Sunny because of his tan and streaked hair. He gave me the occasional wave or grin then seemed to fade into the background again. He was better at it than the others.

Harry drove past in his coupe. Even my lady was there. I wouldn't have seen her unless I'd been specifically looking. She was standing, still as a statue, amongst the undergrowth at the end of the drive.

Connie was parked in the shadow of the trees halfway up to the house. Now that was a surprise. She must have been more shattered by her experience of my abduction than I'd realized. Now Ed wasn't there, she didn't have to hide.

I waved at her and she got out of her car and got into mine. I was so grateful for her presence I picked up her hand, squeezed it and held it in my lap for the rest of the drive.

"You needn't have worried," I said. "You'll know about my guardians. They do their job very well. It's the first time in all those years they've slipped up."

It had suddenly come to me she might have been the one to arrange my protection. I hadn't thought to ask her.

"Guardians?" she looked puzzled.

Perhaps it was better to defer this conversation to another time.

Maurice, muscles straining his white t-shirt, was walking towards us. As usual his expression was grim.

He opened my door then walked around to do the same for Connie. Not a glimmer.

"Morning, Maurice." I said, glancing at my watch to check it was. It wasn't. "I see you were expecting us."

"I'm here in case you need help. A couple of the girls are still here if you want to question them."

"Has anyone else been?"

"Yes, the police but, they left yesterday and haven't been back. And his manager showed up when he saw the newspapers. He shot off and hasn't been here again either. Not seen any of the music people."

"How come you're still here?"

He looked at me with contempt as if it was obvious. Of course it was – he'd want to make sure Ed got his just desserts.

He showed me the way to the study, and Connie and I began to go through the drawers and files. This was so illegal - I might have some fast talking to do later.

I found a file which contained the paperwork for law suits he'd brought against other members of the band. The main focus of his fury seemed to be Jamie and Gil Robson. I couldn't read it now. I'd take it to Grace for her attorney to go through later.

Another file contained personal details on the two brothers. I'd take that too. There were photographs in it.

Then there was the one giving details of the girls who had passed through his grooming process. This, for my purposes, was perhaps the most important.

"Have you done?" asked Connie. "I'll take those back to the car if you want to question the girls."

I passed the files over and walked out to the back of the house where the girls lived.

They weren't a lot of use. They just dithered. They

had been there quite some time and didn't seem bright enough to know what to do next unless someone told them. I gave them what cash I had in my purse, about eighty bucks, and told them to go home. They nodded their heads in unison.

I jumped in the car, put it in gear and left to meet Connie further down the drive. I was just in time to see something which shocked me so much I stuck my foot on the brake, and the car screeched to a halt in a spray of gravel.

Connie was in the process of handing something over to my lady. The latter saw me and faded back into the woodland as if she'd never been. I saw a tow-headed man behind her as she slipped away.

"So what the hell is going on here? What the fuck was that? Do you know her?"

"Slightly. That's Giulia, wife of my first husband. We mentioned her before if you remember, when you heard Grace and I shouting at each other."

"Seems an odd person for you to be friendly with. First and second wives aren't usually on friendly terms. And why has she been stalking me for six years? If you know her, you have to know the answer to that. And if you do, why the fuck haven't you told me?"

"You're right. We're not – friends, that is. And I'm not at liberty to tell you yet. Its someone else's story." Now where had I heard that before.

"I'm going to Grace's to hand over these papers for her attorney to go through. I suggest you go back to Santa Monica and think up your story. If it's going to be another pack of lies and half-truths, you'd better make it a good one. If I could get hold of that slippery snake Giulia, I'd ring her neck. I'll call you when I get to Windham"

"You should be kind to Giulia. Everything that has been done, has been done with love, my darling." And where had I heard *that* before? Were these people working to a script? Even my freakin' parents – the Champaign parents that is. God only knew about the other lot.

"Whatever! But when this is over, there will be some answers."

There was no denying the threat in my voice. I was livid. I was even working myself up to tackle Grace.

Chapter Twenty-Three

The Big Reveal - Part One

I drove to Grace's a week later.

At first she was horrified by what I'd done, but once I'd dropped the files on the table and she'd had a chance to look at them, she shrugged and said:

"You can't use these in court, Christie. They'd jail you for theft. Put them back before anyone notices."

She noted the mulish look on my face and went on.

"However, you have enough personal evidence to land him in jail for a good while. If you could get substantiation from anyone else, that would add to his problems. If you can find someone who could testify to Cindy's incarceration you have him for homicide of one sort or another. Now get those documents back. I'll take a copy for reference first though."

That's my Grace! She didn't want me to break the law but she was willing to stretch things for herself.

"For the blackmail threats. You need to speak to Connie."

Putting the files back was no problem. Grace sent them by next day courier with instructions to put the envelope in Maurice's hands personally and get his signature. Maurice had been left to oversee the estate in Ed's absence, so I rang to tell him of the arrangements.

When asked if he would be prepared to stand up in

court on Cindy's behalf, he showed as much enthusiasm as he was capable of, but he'd suffered so much embarrassment and abuse over the years, he would have testified to pretty much anything. I only wanted him to tell the truth about what he knew of the situation with the young girls at the estate, and what he knew of Cindy's incarceration.

I promised him, in return, I wouldn't press charges for my abduction. He even managed a chuckle. Perhaps his life was on an upswing.

Sorted! No recourse to anyone else. Perfect. I apologized to Grace for my stupidity.

Now to the other matter. Connie was summoned and Grace gave her staff the day off.

To my absolute astonishment, Connie arrived with my lady – Giulia - in tow. I couldn't imagine what that must have cost her in pride. Giulia too. Grace had also asked my parents to be present.

We introduced ourselves, and Grace broke out her best wine as we all sat down round the dining room table. It felt like a diplomatic summit meeting. We all eyed each other suspiciously, waiting for someone to break the silence. It was Connie.

"I kept this from Ed's study," and she slid a photograph across the table. It was of a young couple on their wedding day.

In the photo, the boy was looking at the girl as if she was the most precious person on earth, and she returned his gaze with adoration in her eyes. It was charming.

But what was immediately striking to me was that the girl had straight jet-black hair which fell way below her waist.

"That's me and your father on our wedding day thirty years ago. I was eighteen and he was two years older."

As I was taking this in, it came to my attention that Giulia had tears in her eyes, and my Mom was crying into my Dad's shoulder.

Grace poured the wine. Large measures.

"We separated nine years later and our divorce was finalized three years after that."

"Sorry, can't do the math. Explain. Holy shit! You're my birth mother?" I was incredulous.

"Christie!" demanded Grace, "Lets at least try to keep this civilized. There's a lot more to come. If this shocks you, God help you later!"

Such a comfort, Grace.

"So you're my Mom and Oliver's my Dad."

"No." chipped in Giulia. "My husband is your father."

"So you were up to no good with Giulia's boyfriend after you'd supposedly broken up? Have I got that right?" Connie drew breath to carry on but I held up my hand.

"No. I can't do any more right this minute. I need to fix this in my brain first."

I jumped into Angel and got out of there fast.

I drove down to the flower gardens near Glencoe and sat on the banking of a small lake, idly trying to sink a water-lily leaf with my foot.

Next I knew, Sunny was sitting beside me. He'd never spoken to me before. He'd a Californian accent – but then he would have, wouldn't he, looking as he did?

"Don't be hard on them, Christie. They were very young and very much in love. Life just got in the way," he said with a smile.

I picked up a pebble and aimed it at a perch. Naturally I missed. I watched the water smooth over again then turned back to Sunny, but he was already gone. Damn, he was good!

So, Connie was my birth mother which she'd managed to hide from me for eighteen years. Giulia's husband was my birth father. Grace was the mother of Connie's husband Oliver who, according to that lady, was a bastard – well at least we had that in common – technically anyway..

Simm therefore was Connie's stepson and there was also a daughter, so Oliver must have been married before too. Apart from birth papa, Oliver's former wife was the only person missing. Of course, I'd already known some of this, but it was fascinating, in a detached sort of way, to watch the jigsaw gradually come together.

Time to face the music.

Chapter Twenty-four

The Big Reveal – Part Two

I left the car parked on the road and walked up the drive. Grace had set up her customary cream tea on the lawn. It all looked terribly civilized. They were sipping from delicate china cups and saucers and precariously balancing matching plates on their knees.

Americans are not good at such social niceties. Why should they be? Opening up a continent is done with ploughs and shovels not cucumber sandwiches and Wedgewood. I marched on towards my fate.

Plate-laden, the best they could do was turn their heads and smile at me. Some with love, some with trepidation but most with both.

It was a bit disconcerting to see Grace fuss over me. She got me a chair, put a plate with a couple of sandwiches on my knee which I couldn't then eat because she'd filled my hands with a cup and saucer. I noticed the ones seated away from the table had uneaten sandwiches too.

"Well? Got that in your brain now? Can we continue?" said Grace.

"We can, when you take these out of my hands."

There were sighs of relief all round.

"Can we go back inside? I'll take my sandwiches but a large glass of red would go down better than tea."

"Now, where were we?" said my Illinois Dad, who

also didn't know much of this.

"I have to apologize to Giulia before I go on because I am going to hurt her," said Connie. She looked Giulia in the eye. "This has to be part of the story to make it make sense."

It was easy to see Giulia knew what was coming and it was costing her pain.

"Your father and I were separated, it's true. But it is also true that the love we had for each other had never really gone away."

Giulia stood abruptly and walked over to the window but now she'd started, it was as if Connie was unable to stop.

"Then his beloved brother died. We were both devastated by his loss. He'd always been your father's supporter through difficult times. With him gone, he was adrift. The day after the funeral we both independently went to lay flowers quietly on his grave. To spend a little quiet time with him."

She looked at Giulia and said earnestly:

"I want you to know, Giulia, that the next bit is absolutely the truth.

"We kissed to comfort each other, and he walked away before it got more complicated. It was me who instigated what followed."

She turned back to me and continued:

"We made very passionate love, there in the cemetery." – now wasn't that just dandy? – "and realized, both of us, it was a last goodbye, but you must never, ever believe for a moment you were unwanted."

By this time, all of us were crying, even Grace. In fact, I think Giulia was the most composed of us all. She took over the tale.

"For obvious reasons, Connie and I were adversaries – even though we had known each other from childhood. It was a waste when we both only had the well-being of one extraordinary human being at heart."

Wow! This guy must have been quite something.

"He had always been consumed by his work, and it's true Connie was pushed to the bottom of his list of priorities. Me too, although I think it wasn't as hard for me. Experience had made us both tougher."

It was Connie's turn to walk away. She used the bathroom as an excuse, but everyone knew why she'd really gone. A tense five minutes later she returned.

Giulia resumed:

"Connie became more and more isolated and he increasingly out of control – alcohol and cocaine. The cocaine's gone now but the booze still needs some work. He was being torn in two – both sides of his life were desperately important to him."

"It didn't seem that way at the time," continued Connie. It took my mother-in-law to put me straight. But, in the end it didn't matter. He couldn't make me any less lonely.

"That loneliness was the beginning of new lives for both of us. I would sincerely like to thank you Giulia, for giving him the happiness I couldn't. He got the better end of the deal."

Giulia squeezed Connie's hand across the table. It was

an amazing act of selflessness. Connie took over again.

"Some people pray for years for a baby. You were the result of one single final act of love.

"I couldn't tell your father. I didn't believe he could've dealt with it. But he found out anyway so I had to let him know you'd arrived safely and I'd sent you out of his reach."

"And why, in God's name would you do that?" I asked, dumbfounded.

"Never mind that," said Grace sourly. "You're still too young to know. Just be content with understanding there were good reasons why this all had to be achieved with no paperwork, so neither your father nor the authorities could trace you. What we were doing was highly illegal. Unless everyone was of one mind we could all have been sharing a cell in the penitentiary with your pal, Ed."

I looked at the people who had raised me with more respect. They were truly exceptional for going along with this. It was possible I could have been taken away from them at the whim of strangers. Mom had told me how devastating that would have been.

"Because of this," Connie continued, "I developed an obsession of my own. I determined you would know everything about your father only when you were old enough.

"He is a very engaging character. You would love him – I never knew anyone who didn't. But he thinks everyone is like him which is why he is so often disappointed. Please be strong enough to stand up to him. You are old enough now to be the daughter he desperately needs."

"You should have told me. I had a right to know too – you should have told me.. err.. Connie."

"Nobody told you simply because we believed you would try contacting him. If you did that, no matter how careful you were, he would have found you. Teenagers are not known for their forethought."

I still hadn't a clue what all this was about. There must have been something seriously wrong with him that they were so determined to keep us apart. Perhaps it was the drugs – could he have been part of a cartel? I dismissed this immediately – the thought of Connie married to Pablo Escobar was unthinkable.

"Giulia had the sense to argue him into not trying to see you until you were old enough to make your own decisions intelligently," chipped in Grace, blunt as ever. "He's not stupid. He knew his behavior was the cause of all his problems."

"Despite what happened between us he was, and still is an honorable man," said Connie – not Escobar then - "Sometimes beyond reason. Since he knew of your existence, he has been devastated not to have fulfilled his obligations to you."

She looked to Giulia, who said:

"It's never lessened. He doesn't know you but he has never forgotten - not for a moment."

"It was Giulia's idea to keep tabs on you through your teenage years. Some of his contacts were shifty to say the least," Connie resumed. "I could see her point but thought it was a bit excessive. Turned out she was right though, when Ed came across you and put two and two together." Escobar back in the reckoning?

"Giulia found you through Oliver. He never could contain his jealousy. He kept her informed of your whereabouts regularly over the years, assuming she would pass the information on to her husband. Oliver hated him with a passion – I suppose he thought of this as a way of punishing him."

"Bastard by name, bastard by nature. Not exactly Giulia's caliber," spat his loving mother.

I was sick of this – why couldn't they get to the freakin' point. Were they trying to turn me into a headcase deliberately?

"I STILL DON'T KNOW WHO I AM!"

I slapped my palm down on the table in frustration. Grace glared at me.

"Well," said Connie, unperturbed, "I think it would help if Giulia and I introduced ourselves properly. I am Connie Robson. I adopted the Maxwell name mostly for Simm's sake, but Oliver and I were never married. Apart from anything else, Grace would have had a heart attack."

There was a soft background grunt from Grace.

Connie extended a hand to Giulia:

"And I'm Giulia Robson," she said watching me carefully.

"So my surname's Robson – so what?"

There were deep intakes of breath all round,

especially from Mom and Dad who were mostly as in the dark as I was.

"We were both married to Gil Robson. He was probably a bit before your time but you may know his name."

"WHAT! YOU MEAN MY FATHER IS GIL ROBSON!"

Oh my Lord! That was way better than saying I was sired by Elvis.

He was gorgeous…..well gorgeous in a Dadsy sort of way which made it perfect. And with a voice… what could I say? Wannabe musician that I was, if I was a guy, I'd commit murder for that voice!

What I was thinking must have been plain to see.

"I can't tell you how much he would appreciate your expression at this moment," said Giulia.

"He has zero self-esteem," Connie agreed seriously. "The band robbed him of that over the years – especially Ed and the selfish side of Jamie – believe me he had one. He could be a complete ass."

My Mom shifted slightly in her seat at Jamie's name but these revelations went straight over my head.

"No self-esteem? He's a musical god! Even my generation knows that!"

Giulia looked at me thoughtfully.

"Connie told you that having you looked after for the past six years was my idea. She's right."

She turned to Cathy and Julius, her tone serious:

"There was never any implication that you weren't doing a perfect job of protecting her. But you couldn't be there twenty-four-seven. We had to fill the gaps. Christie will tell you the only people she saw were directly connected with music – you know Bobby of course, and DeeDee Christie's bandmate. Also Harry Forster who had been Gil's friend since their teens."

I wondered about Sunny but it seemed inappropriate to interrupt.

She glanced at Connie before continuing.

"You did know about Bobby, didn't you?"

"No. But I'd have figured it out. Gil was his hero."

"He must be an absolute monster if half the musical world saw fit to put themselves out to protect me from him," I said, digging for more information.

"Oh, don't be such a drama queen," huffed Grace. "Perhaps they were protecting him from you!"

"Bit of both," said Connie. "It's true he's his own worst enemy."

I brightened up:

"Great. When can I speak to him? I can't wait…can he teach me to play an electric keyboard? I've always wanted a go…."

Giulia interrupted my enthusiastic response and so did Mom Cathy's wails. Dad was as white as a sheet. What he dreaded was happening before his eyes. He was losing his baby girl to people he perceived as more interesting. I was immediately contrite:

"I am so sorry, please forgive me. You will always be

my parents – you raised me. Connie and Gil, I hope, will become my friends rather than my parents. That's if I can ever stop thinking of her as Auntie Connie and ever meet him at all."

For the first time – probably since my conception - Connie began to find some humor in the situation. She tried and failed to hide a smile behind her hand.

The relationship between my birth and foster parents was always going to be difficult unless Connie accepted Mom and Dad would always be part of my life.

And I knew she feared for Gil. Past experience had made him vulnerable and she couldn't be sure Giulia would cope. Neither did Giulia from the look on her face.

"When can I see him? I'm bursting with curiosity."

"Of course," said Giulia with sympathy. "But he's very fragile as we said. Can you be patient for just a little while until I can prepare him for meeting you? Emotional shock is not his thing."

"He sounds a bit of a wimp," I said

"No" explained Connie. "It's just that everyone he has loved in his entire life, except his mother and Giulia but including me, has let him down. He adored his brother. Jamie may have died in a accident, but he was already lost to heroin and alcohol. Gil couldn't help him – Jamie wouldn't help himself. Gil came within a whisker of addiction himself more than once.

"Without a doubt, Jamie was lead musician, but Gil held everything together for him for decades. He is exhausted by it. He has had to fight the likes of Ed since he was sixteen years old."

Connie took Grace's hand and, leaning over, kissed her cheek:

"You have an enormous debt of gratitude to pay to Grace. From the day she first held you in her arms you were her granddaughter. Probably why she lets you get away with so much," she said wryly. "She found Cathy and Julius for you and I have to thank her too, for putting up with my frequent hysterics at not seeing you any time I wanted. Thank you Grace – and Julius and Cathy."

My lovely Grace was speechless with emotion.

Everyone rose to leave, donning jackets and collecting purses. As a precaution, telephone numbers were exchanged to be used in an emergency we fervently hoped would never happen.

I still sat at the table numb with shock until Grace told me to clear the glasses into the kitchen.

Chapter Twenty-five
Sweet Simeon

Once the ladies I came to think of as 'the coven' had disassembled, and my poor, overwhelmed Dad with them, I turned to hug Grace.

We'd grown to know more of each other over the past couple of hours than we had before – she now accepted me as an adult, and I saw her as an endlessly indulgent grandmother. I knew, more than that, she would be my closest friend for life.

"Why don't you go to San Clemente to recuperate for a while? You look pole-axed if you don't mind me saying so. I'm sure Simm wouldn't mind. The house is so large you can be alone if you wish," said Grace

"I might take you up on that, Gran," her face was wreathed in smiles. "but first I need to go back to Champaign for a couple of weeks with Mom and Dad - I'd love to go after though."

I could foresee complications here – it was a bit long-winded to call them my Illinois parents and my California parents. Connie, after all this time, just had to stay Connie, so that was no problem – I didn't know about the other one yet. Maybe Gil.

"I'll ring Simm and ask if he minds you staying for a while. But I can tell you now he won't. He's a good boy."

"He's twenty-five! He might object to you calling him

boy."

"Humph! He will always be my little grandson. He knows that."

Once Mom and Dad realized our situation hadn't changed, they were actually quite fascinated by my life history. Mom was bowled over that Jamie Robson's brother was my father. She was so looking forward to meeting Gil.

I pointed out that would be after I met him myself, so it might be a while. She was immediately abashed which was unnecessary. She'd get used to having a world-famous musician in the family. I hoped.

My Dad was ambivalent. He still had his little girl, so he packed his briefcase and went to work.

I spent a few quiet days together with my parents. I caught up with my piano practice, apologized to the band for bailing on them and spent some badly needed me-time sketching.

By the end of the week I'd got myself together again and was actually looking forward to the rest of my life. It suddenly seemed full of exciting possibilities.

I bumped into Harry. He'd been visiting his girlfriend Barbara again and the three of us went to the Uni bar. He'd heard what had happened. I never saw anyone look so relieved in my life.

He told me Giulia had asked him not to mention me to Gil for a little while. More deceit didn't sit well with him, but again he could see the point.

Apart from Giulia and Connie, he probably knew Gil better than anyone, and he thought her approach would be for the best.

I hugged and kissed them both then went back home to pack. I truly felt I had two new friends. Uncle Harry – sounded good.

I told Grace I'd take a taxi from the airport to Los Angeles. She said I wouldn't - Simm would pick me up.

He was his usual sweet self, chatting away in the car on the way back. He told me he'd a couple of friends coming down from LA and they'd be going the few miles to the Trestles to 'catch a wave or two' and would I like to come.

Apart from the occasional jog, I'm a pretty lazy kind of person, so I thanked him and said no thanks. He didn't push it.

"Is it miles away?" I asked.

"Nope. Only three or four miles."

"I might have a walk down then. When will you be coming back?"

"Don't worry about that. I've a rack for the boards and there's only three of us so there shouldn't be a problem. Anyway, one of them can always find his own way back. I won't mind!" he chuckled.

He was so nice. I'd liked him since the first time I met him at this very house, when he came with Connie to see his grandmother Grace.

He helped me out of the car, kissing my hand as he did so. Damn I liked it when he did that! It made my knees go weak. He obviously knew it because he grinned and did it again.

"I won't need to intrude on you. I'll just unpack my bag in one of the guest rooms."

"Oh, intrude away! It's been lonely rattling around in this big old house."

He swung my heavy bag from the car trunk, banged it shut and walked, whistling tunelessly, into the house.

"Front left do?" asked Simm. "It's got a dressing room and shower and you can see right along the beach."

"Sure thing."

He ran up the stairs hefting my heavy bag as if it was as light as a feather and dropped it on the bed.

"See you later then. There's a phone in your room if you need it."

He was so appallingly cheerful I could only assume Grace had given him chapter and verse on my predicament when she called him.

Before he'd got to the bottom of the stairs he'd yelled:

"Christie, I'm going for take-out. What do you want?"

My kinda guy!

"Chinese – chicken chow mein." I shouted back. What was it about this guy that always made me smile?

I unpacked and hung up the couple of dresses I'd brought. Then I rang my Mom and Dad to say I'd arrived safely and to ask how they were.

Mom said I should have a good time, and could I fetch her a fossilized sand dollar if I came across one. Sand dollar? No idea.

"If I come across one, you can be sure I'll pick it up for you."

She seemed content with this non-answer. Dad was as usual, at work and Mom had her round of a state Bridge tournament so she'd to dash.

"Speak later! Be good and have a great time. If one doesn't cancel out the other!" And she was gone.

Next Grace.

"Hi, Gran. I see you gave Simm the full story. He's never stopped whistling and being breezy since I got here. It's quite exhausting. Tell him to quit."

Damn, I sounded more like her by the minute. She must have thought the same as she gave a loud laugh.

"Now why would I do that?" she said.

"He's gone for take-out and we're going surfing tomorrow."

"You are?"

"Well, he is. With a couple of buddies. I'm sitting on the beach, eating ice cream and topping up my tan. I don't have a death wish."

She said she hoped I'd have a good time and said she'd get back to me in a day or two.

Simm came in with the food and requisite fortune cookies and picked up a beer from the cooler on the terrace.

"Want one?" He took another and flipped off the caps.

We sat opposite each other at the dining table, eating with chopsticks out of cardboard cartons. His fortune cookie said, 'take your time', and mine said 'beware a stranger'.

A light breeze from the ocean ruffled his sun-bleached hair. It reminded me of someone momentarily, but I was too distracted to think who. He smiled and his eyes crinkled at the corners and looked brilliant against his deep tan.

Here I was looking at my mother's stepson, dreamy-eyed. What did that make us? Stepbrother and sister? No that couldn't be right. We didn't share blood. Well, that was a relief because what was going through my head had nothing to do with being his sister.

"Are we related?" he said abruptly, as if he'd read my mind.

"Can't be. We don't share a mother or father."

"Good." he said, walked round the table and bent me backwards in a movie-star kiss.

"You can breathe now" he said. I must have been turning blue with shock.

Then the outrageousness of it hit us both at the same time and we laughed.

I walked over to the rail and gazed at the twinkling lights of the town below. The surf moved silver in the moonlight. It was dangerously romantic.

"I'd better go now. I'm tired from the journey. See you in the morning."

He stood gazing down at the tiled floor, hands in his pockets. When he looked up at me his eyes were serious.

"Goodnight" he said. I kissed him on the cheek and left.

The following day was a bit tense. It was easier having his two friends along. They were happy, carefree types as most surfers were, and if they noticed Simm was subdued they said nothing.

Once we arrived, I was left on the sand with an ice cream and a pile of pants, t-shirts and sandals while they all ran off down the beach to do their thing. This wasn't a family beach so there were no children's voices. Just the sound of transistor radios, mostly belting out nostalgia like Dick Dale, Jan and Dean and the Beach Boys.

I was glad I hadn't chosen to go in. My figure didn't bear comparison to the be-thonged bimbettes, giggling along the strand. Seems they didn't have something I did either. A brain.

Simm was a good surfer. He was patient, awaiting the right wave before jumping on his board. The other two were a bit hasty so never caught the really big ones.

While I was ruminating, a boy mounted his yellow board in front of me. I guessed he must have been about sixteen and though he was a distance away I felt he looked straight at me and waved. I stood up for a better view but a wave blew up and obscured my vision. When it retreated there was no sign of him. There was a group of girls about twenty feet away. They must have known him.

He looked a bit like Sunny might have as a boy. But didn't they all?

I finished my cone and went to throw the paper in a near-by bin. When I returned, Simm, dripping, was sitting on a towel on the other side of the pile of clothes.

"Hi," I said, "Good waves?" I cringed inwardly at my stupid question. They were clearly superb. He ignored my remark and continued.

"Christie…. about last night…" I could tell he was embarrassed but determined.

"Think nothing of it. I was as much to blame."

"No, I wasn't going to say that. I wanted to know if…," he took a deep breath. "You would be my girl."

He looked away, red in the face. His demeanor was very un-Simm. Of course it was, he should have been long past this kind of bashfulness.

So, would I? Be his girl, that is. That kiss was pretty mind-blowing.

"Let's date a while before we make that kind of commitment. Don't you think that would be best?"

He avoided by eye and looked back up the beach. I could tell he was disappointed, but he smiled, kissed me on the cheek, grabbed his board and got back in the water.

The young boy on the board rode by, closer this time, but I didn't pay him much mind.

Chapter Twenty-six
Shocks All Round

That evening, after I'd showered and changed, I came down the stairs to the sight every girl dreams of, but rarely sees.

There was a table set for two, with a snowy-white tablecloth and linen napkins. It was decorated with roses and lit by candles. It was so beautiful I gasped. But even more spectacular was Simm, in a tuxedo, glowing from his afternoon's exercise, looking serious and a bit worried. And holding a rose, wisely cream not red. He pinned it to my lapel and whispered softly.

"Too much?"

I couldn't help it. It was so romantic, I just hugged him.

And it went on from there. Dinner was served by a silver service waiter in tails who disappeared discreetly between courses, leaving plenty of time for footsie under the table and lots of eye-gazing above. Candlelight sure does something for twenty-five-year-old guys with blue eyes and sun tans.

We chatted and I hoped afterwards I didn't talk a load of rubbish because I can't remember a single word.

We took the Champagne and a couple of glasses to my room and spent an idyllic night between the sheets.

The following morning he'd gone downstairs and I

tiptoed after him.

He was already showered, dressed and ready for the day. I looked like a train-wreck. So I retraced my steps and put that right, giving my hair a rigorous brushing and plaiting it loosely down my back. Then I adopted a nonchalance I didn't feel and skipped downstairs apologizing for oversleeping et cetera.

The table on the terrace was ready set with coffee and croissants, butter and marmalade. How did he always get it just right?

He kissed me sweetly on the lips and moved to hold my chair for me to sit. He'd no idea how close he came to being embarrassed in front of the servants.

We ate breakfast, each happily wrapped in his own thoughts. A gentle breeze from the sea blew the scent of orange blossom across the terrace.

When we had finished eating, we sat on one of the terrace sofas and finished our coffee.

"I hate to bring the real world into our little paradise," he said, "but we have to consider what we do next.

"We have to explain to Connie that her step-son has hooked up with her daughter. And even more terrifying, tell Grace her granddaughter has been dishonored by Oliver Maxwell's son. That should be interesting."

But he didn't look too concerned.

The phone calls were easier than I thought. We drew straws using coffee spoon handles. He got to call Connie, and I Grace, which is the way round I would have chosen anyway.

I dialed the number for Windham and Annie, Grace's

maid, answered.

"Hello Annie. Is Mrs. Maxwell there please?"

"Good morning, Miss. I'll tell her you're calling if you would hold the line."

"Yes?" said Grace, "Is that you, Christie?"

"You know darn well it is. Annie just told you."

She ignored my response and sailed right on.

"Well, everything okay? Why are you calling at this hour?"

I breathed deeply and looked at Simm for support.

"I just wanted to tell you before anyone else does that…"

"You and Simm are an item. I love it when my plans work out."

She put the phone down. I was lost for words and just gazed at the receiver dumbfounded.

I couldn't stop Simm laughing, he wept with it. When he started choking, I'd to bang him on the back and bring a glass of water.

Next, Connie. Either she'd love us or hate us.

It was hard to tell which from the next ten minutes, through the sobs. My Lord, that woman could cry for America. But finally, we managed to get the idea she was pleased. Her major concern was breaking it to the rest of the family – especially Gil. I couldn't see how this would be a problem. We weren't even acquainted yet.

"Couldn't Uncle Harry break it to him? He seems to trust him."

"Who?" said Connie, blankly.

"Uncle Harry…. Harry Forster. You know. Do concentrate Connie!"

"Now now, Christie – that's no way to speak to you mother!" said Simm, gleefully.

"Thank you, Simeon. That was very kind," said Connie who couldn't see his face.

I scowled at him and mouthed 'creep'.

I'd forgotten Cathy and Julius. Simm became serious. I couldn't imagine why. Compared to Grace they were pussycats.

"How do you think they'll take it?" he asked. "Will they think I'm okay?"

"Let me put it this way. My last serious boyfriend smoked pot, chased me over the University lawns then acted inappropriately while I was high. And they like him so I guess you won't have much of a problem."

There was slight poetic license there for effect.

"The bastard!" he said, offended. "What did you do?"

"Pretty much what you'd expect from a sixteen-year-old, I guess. I told him I would love him forever and ever. That lasted about a month if that."

The following day we drove up to the estate I'd been held captive on. I wanted to see Maurice and make sure the files had been returned okay.

Despite the fact he'd manhandled me so badly, I knew there was no evil intent. Ed gave him jobs to do and he did them. He'd learned from long experience it was better to overdo a job than the reverse.

Ed was capable of great cruelty as his indictment on charges of manslaughter proved. His bail had been set at fifty million dollars. I didn't understand the niceties of the legal process but understood, even if found guilty, appeals through various courts could take years, during which time he'd be incarcerated. That'd do for now.

Maurice and some of the other staff were still intent on standing up in court. Many others were too scared. Maurice had been in touch with the families of a couple of the girls who were willing to testify also.

The estate was in the process of being mothballed and Maurice was one of the last ones there. I asked what he intended to do when his contract ended. I could tell only by a slight tick in the muscle of his cheek what he was thinking. He was worried.

He was divorced but had custody of his two kids who were in high school locally. He'd prefer not to interrupt their education but he'd to go where he could find work.

All the time we'd been speaking, Simm had been sitting on a low wall listening intently.

He was very quiet on the drive back to San Clemente and I could tell he was chewing something over.

As we walked through the house, after he'd dropped his car keys in a bowl by the front door – a habit he'd picked up from Connie – he said:

"What do you think Grace would say to employing Maurice to oversee this place? She's away a lot of the time. Also she's an elderly lady – no don't deny it. She is. San Clemente is pretty good for crime rates but it's tempting fate for her to be alone here. Her jewelry and money are kept in a safe in the library but there's so many antique bits and pieces. I'd guess she has no clue what it's all worth."

"Well, good luck convincing her she's a vulnerable old lady. Let me know in advance so I can sell tickets. The whole of Illinois and half of California would pay good money for that."

"Of course, you're right. And I realize she has staff but there's only a couple who sleep in and they're both women. They couldn't fight off an intruder. Maurice could. He could also organize the outdoor staff."

I subconsciously rubbed my right eye where that gentleman's manhandling had damaged my face and finally agreed.

"She's awkward enough to take a shine to him. I'll tell her I have a surprise for her. Gets her every time."

Simm was grinning to himself, obviously at past memories.

What I said next came as a complete surprise, especially to me.

"I love you, Simm. I really do."

My hand flew to my mouth. Goddam, where did that come from? My cheeks were scarlet.

I'd scared myself, not to mention Simm, to death.

"Wow," he said.

"Oh, my God," I replied and bolted for the door.

PART TWO
Giulia's Thoughts

Chapter One
Leader of the Pack

It had been a grueling, but long over-due meeting and I was surprised at how much common ground Connie and I had managed to find.

Christie's adopted parents were lovely kind people completely overwhelmed by Grace. Cathy was very emotional. She was just so terrified of losing the little girl she'd cared for from babyhood. My heart went out to her.

The awful truth *I* had to come to terms with was that while he'd learned to live without Connie at a heart-breaking cost, he would always love her. He'd given his heart at eighteen and never got it back again. Christie's conception was not a surprise to me, although I often shed bitter tears over it later.

Our own relationship was more complicated - a cross between father-daughter and husband-wife. He was ten years older than me and sometimes I think he felt it. Also, the stress of his life had told on him, worn him down.

Which is why what happened next was so important.

I went home to Colorado. The house was empty apart

from the housekeeper. I would usually have been with Gil, who was in England, but I used Giordano family matters as an excuse to cover my absence. My father had recently been diagnosed with renal problems and was refusing point blank the necessary surgery, so it was believable.

A fire had been lit in the sitting room for my arrival, and a light snack laid out on an end table next to the sofa. I couldn't eat but I drank coffee and smoked a cigarette.

I didn't sleep well that night. The events of the past few days played over and over in my brain. I was up at dawn and watched the sun rise over the Rockies from the cathedral room. As always, it was breathtaking, and temporarily washed all my problems away.

I had bought the house for Gil before we were married. The mountains were the only place he truly relaxed.

The cathedral room was named for its soaring ceiling. One wall was entirely of glass and gave an uninterrupted view of the peaks. Gil would never have it covered, saying he could still see the glow of moonlight on the mountain peaks even in the dead of night. But I think he felt rather than saw them.

The room was too cold for me. It was so big it was impossible to heat properly. Gil had a full-sized white grand piano he'd had imported from Italy there, and various other keyboards too large for his cottage at the bottom of the drive.

I would often find him wrapped in a robe, guitar resting on his knee, gazing outside. There had been a few conifers obscuring the view, so he had them cut down.

Sometimes, friends would come by and write lyrics with him there. He enjoyed their company. He was especially happy to see Harry Forster and David Elliot who had helped him through some bad times.

Three of them together - replacement brothers perhaps? Happily, Harry and David were nothing at all like Jamie, although it would have been a mistake to say that to Gil.

Harry had helped me so much when it came to surveillance for Christie. I set this up originally to watch out for her safety and so I could determine the best time to bring her back into Gil's life.

I was always acutely aware this often went against the grain with Harry, who was tender hearted and very sensitive to others. But he went along with it for Gil's sake. David would have nothing to do with it at all. I was sad about that but respected his decision.

Bobby, my other musketeer, was Connie's brother. There were a few years spanning Connie's divorce, when he didn't think it would be appropriate for him to be around Gil for his sister's sake, but that was all. So Gil won that one too, although any bad feeling between brother and sister had evaporated long ago.

And the final spy was Deedee, Bobby's current girlfriend who once sang in the same band as Christie. She came late to the team but was conveniently close to Christie when the rest of us couldn't be.

Then there was me. Meeting Christie was a crushing

The Twinkle in Pa's Eye

experience. I wanted to dislike her from pure and simple jealousy. But she was such a sweetheart, bright as a button at thirteen.

She was very lovely: a perfect combination of Gil and Connie's best features. She'd Connie's stupendous hair, high cheekbones and tip-tilted velvet eyes, and Gil's nose and mouth. Combined, her features outmatched both of her parents. She loved the dew-drop diamond bracelet Gil bought for me when we were young. On her wedding day, I will give it to her.

I only spoke to her once more, in a theatre foyer when she seemed particularly sad. She was older then and aware we were following her. I knew she wanted to talk to me, so I offered what comfort I could and disappeared before she could question me further.

Gil would be so proud of her. She was clever, artistic, beautiful and Bobby said she was a very talented pianist. Now just how to tell him about her.

After Jamie died Gil struggled on, but Ed beat the heart out of him. Thank God for Harry and David. They picked him up and got him back in the studio. But that was only a small part of the problem.

He loved his fans with a passion - they gave him a reason for being. There was a song he sang only for them, and they knew it and called for it at every show. That drove Ed wild. It was the only time, in later days, Gil ever smiled on stage.

It was the sweetest smile I ever saw.

It is a dreadful thing to say, but Gil's best stroke of luck came with Ed going to jail. The band wanted him back. Truth be told, it came as a relief. It was his métier and he felt secure there, but it could only be a temporary measure. He was no longer young and tired easily.

Gil was due to fly into Denver the following morning. I packed an overnight case and put it in the back of my car. My Dad had bought me an apartment block in Denver for my twenty-first. According to him, it was so I could learn about business. Such an untruth - it was just indulgence.

We'd stay there overnight and travel home the next morning.

I had offered to pick him up but he said it would be easier to take a cab. I suppose it was, but I would have been happy to pick him up anyway.

When he arrived, he was gray in the face from fatigue. I recognized the signs - if I didn't get him into bed soon, he'd collapse.

His blood pressure had soared in recent years. It didn't help that he'd put on a lot of weight. He'd had that problem his entire life. As in so many other aspects of his life, he'd just given up. The pounds had piled on.

The concierge took his suitcase from the cab, and I helped support him into the elevator and opened the door to the apartment.

He flopped down into an armchair and I bent to untie his shoelaces, but in a breathy whisper, he said:

"No, don't do that yet. Just let me sit for a moment. Can you fix me a coffee?"

He tipped his head back on the chair and closed his eyes. This time the headache was bad.

I fixed his coffee and came back with an ice pack for his head and a sandwich. He grimaced at the salad filling but said nothing. He'd lost thirty pounds and had about the same to go.

He loved that he was beginning to turn heads again. Me, not so much. He'd always been a handsome man with a devastating smile. The girls would tear Jamie's clothes from his body, but Gil had a more subtle, enduring charm.

He clutched his head from the pain.

"Please, if you don't mind, I'd like to rest until tomorrow. Today is not good. I'm getting too old for all this travelling. I'm just so tired."

"Why don't you just quit? We have more than enough to live well on for the rest of our lives."

"Tomorrow, we'll talk about it tomorrow" he said wearily, and dragged himself to bed.

As each obstacle was resolved another would rear its head. I had a feeling the secret I had held from him all these years could rapidly become yet one more.

Presently, his own father was suing him over some song rights. Gil didn't give a damn who owned the songs he sang.

While this wrangle was ongoing, he was missing out on singing for his fans. He always called them 'friends' – perhaps they were. Many of them had been there for him when he was at his lowest.

The following morning, I tied on an apron and cooked my husband his very favorite breakfast. He was supposed to be on a perennial diet, but today I'd cut him a break. He needed cheering up.

The smell of breakfast cooking was always the best way to shift him from his bed and this morning was no exception. He wandered in as I was turning the bacon, wrapped his arms around me and nibbled my earlobe.

"Mornin' wife. Where's my oatmeal smoothie? Isn't that a bit much for one little person on her own? Or are we expecting guests?"

I flicked the spatula at him and he laughed. These lovely intimate moments had become increasingly rare lately.

"I see you're feeling better this morning. Sit down. Coffee coming up."

I dished up his breakfast and sat across the table while he ate. He was a cook's dream – an appetite second to none. Sadly.

"When are you playing Anaheim again?" I asked.

"A week Thursday. Why?"

"Oh nothing. I just fancied a night out with some friends and there's this okay band playing there a week Thursday."

"I'll book a suite for you. Is that what you'd like?"

"I'll get back to you."

Chapter Two

Anaheim

We drove back home to Colorado later that day. Such a wonderful journey, the air crisp and smelling of snow on the peaks above.

The closer we got to home, the more Gil relaxed. As I pulled the car into our drive, he began to sing the lovely melody which always awoke his soul on the last stretch of the journey home:

".... asked me how I knew

My true love was true...."

Hearing him sing this always made the hairs on the back of my neck stand up. His voice would soar to the tops of the overhanging conifers and hover there in the air before melting into the ether. I believed, and still do, there was nothing closer to heaven on earth than hearing Gil Robson sing in these mountains.

He felt it himself in a different way. The look in his eyes would alter and it was plain to see he was transported to another plane. In this he was so lucky, and his blessing was he knew it.

I pulled in front of the house and listened to him finish the song. As usual, on that last ringing note, he was staring at the mountains, moist eyed.

He'd once told me it was in the snow near Anasazi

Village, where the studio used to be, he last spoke to Jamie. But as Jamie had been dead by then, I took it for his fancy, his loneliness. When I said so, he just turned away as if he didn't expect me ever to understand. But I did – or at least I'd thought so.

And as usual, as soon as we entered the house, he put on the heating and lit the fire laid in the cathedral room. He spent ten minutes lighting candle after candle on sconces. They fluttered and danced in the draught from the chimney. Shadows deepened and the softly glowing light caught the strands of silver in his hair and beard. Every now and then he glanced out of the huge plate glass window. His reflection glimmered back at him through points of soft light.

He blew on his fingers against the cold and began to restring a new acoustic, sitting cross-legged on the floor, instrument rested across his knees.

It didn't last long, perhaps a half hour, but in that time the whole world, with me in it, ceased to exist for him. Every time we came home it was the same. It always led to me unpacking his case and putting everything away feeling bereft.

I'd often wondered about Connie. That he loved her still was a fact he'd always freely admitted to me. But at our discussion, she's said she'd left him because she couldn't live with the loneliness. She'd told me he was connected to music and his audience so absolutely there was no place for her.

It was my choice to stay. He knew that and was immeasurably grateful. In our own ways we were content, if not happy.

Another conundrum for me was the way Gil connected with his two boys, now well into their twenties. They didn't seem to permeate his consciousness in the same way as the adults in his life. They were there, he saw them occasionally, they had been here to stay in school vacations. Mylo even lived with us for a while before he went off to college.

My own family life had always been idyllically happy. My mother could be a dragon but never, ever to her close family. My father was ridiculously indulgent, especially to me, the baby of the family, and my brother's over-protective attitude drove me mad.

Gil's family was so different. He refused to talk about his father at all and his beloved mother was often too concerned with looking after Gil's older son Jacob, who doted on her.

His own brother was dead in mysterious circumstances and before that at times hadn't even realized Gil was there.

Oddly, Gil seemed to connect more with Jamie's children than his own. Perhaps it was because he missed his brother so much.

My thoughts turned to the situation with Christie and, the more I considered it, the more worried I became.

Had what I'd done been wrong? What I had done, he could misconstrue as deceit if he was upset. I had persistently lied to him when I had to be away. All these years later, would he understand why? How would he feel about Christie? I just didn't know and it made me nervous.

"Do you still want the suite at Anaheim?" Gil asked, kissing me on the cheek.

"I'll let you know this afternoon. Okay?" I raised up on my toes and kissed him full on the lips.

Sometimes our lovemaking made him uncomfortable, as I think he'd never really let go of the notion I was still a child. Sometimes, if I was especially demanding, he'd respond in kind. He was a passionate man who enjoyed physical love. Complicated as I said.

"Don't leave it any longer – they snap up quickly and it's going to be a sell-out."

"Okay"

His attention drifted back to his guitar. He relit a couple of the candles which had died and sank to his knees with his ear to the strings the better to pick up the resonance. He was lost to me. In this particular instance, that was not a bad idea.

I grabbed my purse and walked as quickly as I could to the kitchen phone, which was furthest away from where he sat.

I dialed Grace's number and waited impatiently, tapping my fingernails against the marble countertop. I got her answerphone, so I tried again.

"C'mon, c'mon, come on." I chanted impatiently, "C'mon, pick up."

I covered the mouthpiece with my hand and glanced up the hall. Still all clear.

The phone clicked and a voice at the other end said

"Yes? Who is it?" She'd answered the phone herself which was not usual.

"Grace, Its Giulia. Do you have a few minutes to speak?" I whispered down the line.

"What's wrong with your voice?" she asked at the top of her lungs. She was an awkward old harridan.

"Shh! He'll hear you?"

"Who'll hear me?" she bellowed. I don't think she did really - it's just she wasn't being quiet either.

"Gil." I breathed, hoping she'd catch on.

"Oh Gil. Why didn't you say so to begin with – it took you long enough."

I rolled my eyes. This was Connie's "mother-in-law" and no relation at all, but she seemed to have taken full responsibility for all things Christie.

"I'd like to invite Christie to one of Gil's shows. Incognito of course. Do you want to come as well? It's a week Thursday at Anaheim."

"Is Connie going?" She was trying my patience now.

"Of course not! I can't sit in the audience with my husband's first wife. Apart from anything else, he'd think we were plotting something."

"You are." Grace pointed out.

"Yes…. well…oh, never mind." I hung up in a temper.

Within minutes she'd rung me back.

"Don't get on your high horse!" she snapped. "What do you want?"

"As I said, Gil has booked a suite for us for the show at Anaheim Thursday week. Would you and Christie like to come?"

"Love to. Where shall we meet you?"

"Don't you think you should check with Christie first?"

"Do you really think she's going to pass up a chance to hear her father sing?"

No, I supposed not.

"What about Julius and Cathy?"

"Oh, I think seeing Gil would be their worst nightmare of a social event!"

"I'll send the passes for you to get in the stadium. Be there about seven"

"Okay." Down went the receiver again.

"Well, goodbye to you too."

That was the hard bit. Easier was inviting the rest of them:

Harry Forster and his fiancé Barbara, Bobby with Deedee who used to sing in Christie's band and Gil's old friend David Elliot, girlfriendless for the first time in his life.

That made eight. Perfect. And Christie would get to meet all of her guardians at the same time.

Gil had had ten days off. I walked with him in the mountains once or twice but he could go further and faster than I could. I left him alone after a day or two to enjoy the solitude.

Two days before the show, we travelled to Anaheim and stayed in a rented suite at a nearby hotel. The rehearsals were grueling as usual, but without Ed, Gil was far happier.

I saw the final sound checks before I went to meet my guests. Gil was in very good voice and the sidemen happy and enthusiastic.

The rest of the guys in the band hugged as they arrived which was a first – that I'd seen in any case. Gil's guitars were being tuned by one of his technicians and the ones he'd picked out put on conveniently placed stands.

This was going to be a good show.

Chapter Three

Star Struck

I met our guests at the suite door.

I'd already had the catering staff lay out some snacks and a couple of bottles of wine. There was a sitting area behind the auditorium seats. It was an hour before showtime. Gil was fully occupied.

Bobby and Deedee turned up first. While Bobby was reticent, his girl never stopped chattering. Clearly she was excited about the evening. That made me like her.

Christie had been staying at Grace's San Clemente home with Connie's stepson Simeon Maxwell. Grace, I'd deduced, was nothing if not theatrical. She timed it perfectly. The last to arrive by three minutes.

Christie looked beautiful. She'd plaited strands of her raven hair with silver ribbon and wound them round her head like a coronet. The rest of it fell in a waterfall below her waist. She wore tight jeans and a short, sequined top which looked exactly right on her. I couldn't resist it. I took off the silver charm bracelet I was wearing and clasped it round her right wrist. It matched her outfit perfectly and tinkled as she moved.

Grace was her usual arrogant self but looked with approval at the bracelet. She shook hands with the rest of my guests rather stiffly, then relaxed slightly when offered a glass of chilled Sauvignon.

I introduced David to Christie as – with Harry - her father's oldest and dearest friend. I explained that although Harry had watched over her all this time for Gil's sake, Gil had known nothing about it. David grunted his disapproval.

Deedee chattered on in her groovy fashion, and eventually Christie slipped back into their friendship again.

"Where's Sunny?" Christie asked, looking round.

"Who?" said Harry and David in unison.

"That's a name I've given him. I don't know his real one. He's been watching me too, but I've only spoken to him once." She turned to Grace. "The day you told me about Gil and I ran off and sat in the park at Glencoe. He explained to me about Connie and Gil."

"Nope. Don't know who you mean," said David

I found it very disturbing that someone no-one else knew, including Grace, had been following her?

"What's this, Christie?" demanded Grace.

"It's no big deal," Christie said impatiently." I suppose if he'd meant me any harm, he'd have had plenty of time and opportunity. I just thought he was one of you, especially as I saw him walking with Giulia a couple of times."

I shivered. What was she talking about? I knew no Sunny.

At that moment the band was announced on stage and the cheering began. Glasses in hand, we took our seats, looking down on a sea of upturned faces.

Since Ed had left, there was no strutting self-aggrandizement to open the show, for which I was profoundly grateful.

Gil launched into a prolonged guitar solo, and John took over the lead, with Gil providing the harmony. It was one of the old songs from when Gil was eighteen and which he'd hated ever since. But the fans liked it, so he played it anyway.

Song after song increased the frenzy in the crowd below. The fans gyrated and shouted the words, in unison with the band. I always thought it must have looked terrifying from the stage, but Gil loved it. He only seemed fully alive when confronted by 'his friends'.

Then the stage lights went down, and Gil stood alone in a spotlight's glow. I looked at Christie. She didn't know it yet, but this was to be the highlight of her life to date. He looked directly into the audience and smiling that heart stopping smile he didn't know he possessed, looked down at his guitar then walked to his mic.

To someone who has never heard it, his voice was difficult to describe. It had a register which moved from baritone to high tenor and it was like cream, smooth and liquid. The crowd was silent as the notes soared high into the starry sky above the stadium.

Christie had moved to the front of her seat, her mouth slightly opened in disbelief, her eyes full of tears. This was the father she'd never known and may *never* know unless I found a way. I *would* find a way. This profound kind of love could be the saving of him.

Harry must have read my face because he put an

understanding hand on my arm.

Even Grace was dumbstruck.

At the end of the song, he looked full into the eyes of members of the audience and bowed, smiling. He thanked them for coming to see them. The crowd went wild and cheered and cheered.

In that instant, Gil glanced momentarily in our direction. He nodded briefly and returned his attention to the audience. Grace's hands tightened on the box surround. The spotlight faded.

There were other solos sung by other singers which the audience clapped and sang along to, but for us the evening belonged to Gil. Especially for Christie. I found her sitting on a couch in the rest room, sobbing her heart out.

I cuddled her until her tears stopped and she whispered:

"I don't care how you manage it, Giulia, but I have to meet him – even if he doesn't know who I am."

"I promise I will fix it somehow. But it can't be now. He will recognize you instantly. You are the image of your mother at the same age."

**Christie looked so miserable as if she'd been rejected.

"I know he will love you. Don't doubt that for a moment. You are everything he would want in a daughter, even down to the piano playing."

She smiled tentatively.

The Twinkle in Pa's Eye

I thought of the times before Gil and I were together. He'd told me, that if he'd a daughter, he would like her to be just like me.

"Come on now. Let's join the others." I said to her and

dug some tissues out of my bag, dabbed her eyes and wiped her beautiful face. She hugged me close then kissed me on the cheek.

"Thank you. Thank you so much for giving my father back to me. I wouldn't have minded if he'd worked in Walmart. He'd be mine." Then she started to laugh. "Naturally I'd prefer him to be Gil Robson who can sing like a lark. But then I'm naturally greedy."

The other guests were packing up to leave. There were hugs and kisses and promises of other meetings exchanged.

Grace had been strangely silent. She didn't know Gil, had never met him. All she knew had come through Connie. But Connie never spoke ill of him. Few people did.

I asked her if she was okay. Christie put her arms round the lady she thought of as her grandmother. She'd much of Gil about her. He loved to touch people too.

It took Grace a few moments to respond. I'd never heard her stuck for words before. She appeared distracted.

"What's wrong, Gran?" asked Christie, concerned. "Are you feeling okay?"

"Oh, I'm fine. Don't fuss!."

Back to normal!

"I was always told your father was a 'pop singer' – like David Cassidy or Johnny Ray." *Johnny Ray?* "But your father sings exquisite music like an angel, Christie. This was praise indeed from Grace. "I might even go see him again."

"Gran!" exclaimed Christie, "let's not go over the top!"

These two were a perfect pair.

Chapter Four

Catastrophe and Confrontation

Christie flew back with Grace to Chicago and then on to Champaign. I didn't expect to see her for a little while. It would give me time to think about her and Gil. At the moment I could think of no way to be gentle with him. Perhaps I was being oversensitive. But the disaster of his marriage to Connie still made me hold back.

I had given Christie my phone number but asked her only to call in an emergency.

One day the phone rang, and Gil answered it. A very panicked Christie said:

"Is Giulia there? Please I need to speak to her urgently. Urgently!" The last word was shouted down his ear.

"Honey – there's someone on the phone for you. Urgent, apparently."

An emergency of monumental proportions had blown up within the month.

Grace had had a stroke. A severe one.

She'd been discovered in bed by her maid when she took up her morning tea. She was unable to talk, rigid, and with saliva running from the corner of her distorted mouth. The maid was very young, but thankfully had the sense to call 911 and Grace was rushed to hospital.

Little Annie, the maid, hadn't known who to call. She didn't know many of Grace's associates, but she did know Connie and Christie. It was Annie who called Christie to tell her what had happened.

My gorgeous husband was standing over me holding the phone and smiling at me expectantly. How the hell was I going to tell him about this without mentioning the word 'Maxwell'?

"It's one of the women who came to your show - she's had a stroke. She has a house in San Clemente. I'll have to go - her granddaughter is in a real panic."

Gil took the receiver out of my hand, replaced it on the phone and put the phone back on the kitchen worktop. He held me tight and kissed the top of my head.

"Of course you should go. I'll ring the airport and book you a flight to LA as soon as possible. Go get your things together."

Oh my God, I so hated lying to him.

Gil dropped me at the airport. On the concourse, I cancelled the ticket he'd reserved and bought one for Chicago.

I rang Grace's number before I got on the plane. Her grandson answered and I asked for Christie.

"On my way, Christie. I'll be there as soon as I can. It'll be about three hours. I'll get a taxicab from the airport."

"No. Simm'll pick you up. One of us has to stay here in case the hospital calls and he could do with a distraction."

It seemed the panic was off. Christie was in control again.

Simm was lovely but very jumpy, which was understandable. He drove back so fast that when he got a ticket, he drove off down the road at the same speed he'd been stopped for.

Christie met us at the door and it very quickly became apparent she and Simm were an item.

He took my bag and put it in one of the guest rooms while Christie explained the situation. Her parents had offered to come over but as they hadn't really known Grace, they thought they might just be in the way. Christie must have been relieved they were only a couple of hours away if she needed them.

I pointed out that I didn't really know Grace at all, but she said as I was her step-mother - Oh my God! – she'd hoped I'd come. She needed the moral support and Simm was little or no use in the state he was in.

Connie was unwell and hadn't been able to get away immediately but was expected the following day.

Christie wanted me to go with her to the hospital. Simm couldn't face it at that time.

Meanwhile, unbeknown to me, all my carefully laid plans had begun to unravel. I pieced together later what had happened, but it went something like this. It was worse than I could possibly have imagined.

Gil had with little difficulty obtained the number and called the house at San Clemente to check I had arrived safely. The phone was answered by the caretaker who told him no-one was there at present.

"Surely there must be some mistake," puzzled Gil, "My wife is there – Giulia Robson?"

"I'm sorry Sir. There's nobody here by that name. Miss Christina and Mr. Simeon, the only ones who were here, have returned to Illinois to be with Mrs. Maxwell after her stroke. I believe Mr. Oliver and his fiancé are to join them"

Fiancé? Gil had been astounded. He needed to find out what was going on. Simeon - hadn't that been the name of Oliver Maxwell's little boy? – well, not so little anymore.

The caretaker, totally innocent of any implications, gave Gil Grace's address. He jumped on a plane straight to Chicago, picked up a hire car and arrived in Windham, exhausted, shortly after we'd all gone to bed.

Christie opened the door to his loud knock. What could she do but let him in?

Gil's mouth fell open in shock. He was looking at his first wife when she was a teen. Right down to the midnight hair and stunning eyes. He sat down on a hall chair hard.

"Who are you?" he finally managed to gasp.

What was the point of lying when the truth was so evident? I stood at the top of the stairs listening with increasing horror as Gil was hit square-on by his long-lost daughter and my deceit.

"I'm Anna Christina Heywood - Christie…..your daughter." I saw her look heavenward as she said it.

He fell apart before our eyes. I ran down the stairs in my robe and tried to reach him, but he was already out of the door and driving off the way he'd come.

Christie looked at me, shamefaced.

"I couldn't think of a lie. What you said was true. By his reaction, I must have been Connie's image at the same age."

"That's not your fault. Stay here with Simm and see to Grace. I'll go and try to effect some damage limitation. Before I leave, may I use the phone? I need to call Harry. Gil might go to his mother's home in Los Angeles."

I took the diary from my purse and read out a list of numbers to try while I travelled home. Nancy, Liz, John, Todd his studio technician, Bobby – there were more. Surely he must be with one of them.

Harry met me off the plane. Bobby and Davy were with him. They hadn't seen Gil. They'd tried every number on my list plus some of their own. No joy. He'd disappeared into thin air.

PART THREE
In which Father and Daughter Connect

Chapter One

Knee-jerk Reaction

Gil

Christie – my little girl's name was Christie – my daughter and the double of her mother. There could be absolutely no doubt. At the sight of her my brain had stopped working. Everything I did afterwards was a reflex.

It was the middle of the night when I got to Denver. My nerves were in tatters.

I grabbed a hire car and headed straight home to Riverside. There had been a snow flurry during the day, enough to blanket the roads and frost the conifers over the drive. It had slowed me down a little, so I left the car and picked up my SUV.

I threw a few items into a sports bag, pulled on a parka and some walking boots, and headed out into the night without a clue where I was going. The phone had been flashing a message, but I didn't want to talk to anyone – especially Giulia.

Alone. I needed to be alone where no-one would find me, for the time being at least.

I slipped on ice on the doorsteps and fell on my face on the drive, blood gushing from my nose. I tried to stand but had to drag myself upright against the house wall.

Stars blinked and twinkled down at me from a blue-black sky. Blue-black like her hair. My stomach heaved with the blood I'd swallowed.

Eventually the bleeding eased, and I could think again. Where to go where no-one would find me?

Anasazi. The old studio had been sold off years ago, but the building where Jamie had been working on his masterpiece album when he died, was a ruin of upright planks, jagged and roofless from a devastating fire. A building where I'd made my best music with dear friends, now a burnt-out shell. I'd promised Jamie in my heart I'd get his album finished and issued but I never had.

It was where I had last spoken to him, dead for over twenty years. Jamie. I wiped my nose on the back of my hand. It came away bloody.

I had only gone a few miles in my Land Rover when the road began to swim before my eyes, and I nearly swerved into a ditch.

Apart from a half hour snatched on the plane, I hadn't slept in forty-eight hours. So, I parked up in the shelter of some overhanging branches, grabbed an old blanket I'd stowed in the back and settled down to sleep. My breath came in puffs of vapor from the cold. I daren't run out of fuel on this dirt back-road so I didn't use the heater.

I managed a couple of hours of uneasy sleep but then had to get out of the car and run up and down the road to get the blood flowing to my frozen hands and feet.

I sat in the Land Rover with the engine running for the heater for just a few minutes until I was fit to drive.

Anasazi in the moonlight, its ruins black against a black sky – ruins, sky, hair, all black.

The ground was hard and rutted from the cold.

This was a dangerous place to be alone at night. There were mountain lions and bear, and I had no gun. I just hoped some of the cabins were still intact.

Oddly, the only cabin which had remained whole was the Snowliner, where I'd stayed before with Jamie and once, when Connie and I had finished it all. Both times to escape from myself.

The same as this, in fact.

Paranoia caused me to hide the SUV behind the cabin.

It had just been abandoned with everything rotting inside, covered with dust and spiders' webs. But there was wood in the lean-to and the pot-bellied stove was intact. Wonder of wonders – I found a can of baked beans in a cupboard and a knife to open it.

I lit the stove and basked in its warmth. Within minutes I was fast asleep.

When I woke, I heated the beans in their can on the fire and devoured them off the knife.

I couldn't resist climbing the mountain slope and sitting on the same rock as I had so many desperately lonely years ago.

Connie had once said it didn't matter who you were with through the day, just so long as you had someone to go home to at night. I had so rarely been there at night for her. Our marriage had died from suffocation.

I returned to the cabin's warmth. It was only then I allowed myself to think over what had happened.

I'd known I had a daughter, but she was not real to me until now. And she was even more beautiful than her mother. I hadn't thought that was possible. I knew her adopted name now so I should be able to learn more.

But why bother when I could simply ask her? Perhaps I should just go home.

I was angry with Giulia, but there was no real reason. It may have just been that she'd known Christie when she was being kept from me. But I should do her the courtesy of asking.

I passed Giulia driving along the back road. She turned around and followed me home.

Every light was burning in the house, and I could see people moving around. I just couldn't do this right now.

When Giulia had gone into the house, glancing at me as she went by, I got back into the SUV and drove to a nearby roadhouse, ate something and slept. I ought to have felt better but I didn't.

By five am I was back on the road and flying to LA.

Chapter Two
A Sad Farewell

Christie

Giulia had said she'd come with me to the hospital to see Grace, but circumstances dictated otherwise.

Simm had gone to pieces. His grandmother had been his prop through some very tough times. The thought of her not being there was more than he could bear. He ran me to the hospital but couldn't get out of the car. He would not be comforted so perhaps a little time on his own was what he needed most of all.

The paramedics had rushed Grace to the nearest medical facility, where she would remain for a week until she was stabilized, before moving her to the specialist stroke hospital in Chicago.

Fortunately for Grace, Annie had found her almost immediately and she was receiving treatment within the vital first three hours.

I pitied the hospital staff. At the best of times, she was never going to be an easy patient, but the doctors explained there could be behavioral alterations including aggression and depression should she survive.

For Grace's sake, I hoped she didn't. She would hate it. This stroke was severe enough to tie her to a wheelchair for life.

The doctors didn't want to say anything further until she'd been seen by a specialist in Chicago.

They wouldn't let me see her just yet as she was

undergoing intensive treatment but suggested a visit in two days' time.

There was nothing to do but spend a very painful couple of days trying to do what I could for Simm.

I pointed out she hadn't died, she'd had a stroke. But he only repeated the conclusion I'd come to myself.

"But it may not come to that." I said sympathetically. "The doctor also told me there was no way of knowing the rate of recovery or the amount of function she could regain. We'll have to wait and see and do what we can for her in the meantime."

It would be a while before either of us could admit, even to ourselves, she was finished. Life without Grace was just unimaginable for us both.

But, on top of all this, I had my father to consider – my California one that is.

What damage had I done to him? Wasn't it my fault as Giulia had said or could I have behaved differently to make it easier for him, and everyone else. I couldn't have done anything about my appearance and that was what clinched it.

He'd disappeared completely. The last Giulia had seen of him was on a dirt road close to the house. She'd no idea where he'd been but, when they'd both driven back home, he waited for her to go inside then backed up with a screech of brakes and fled.

One of the staff had thought they'd seen his car in a local motel on her way to work but couldn't be sure. By the time they'd gone to investigate, the manager recognized the description but said he'd left in the early hours and not been back. They paid his bill.

Giulia had called her apartment building in Denver, but her concierge hadn't seen him.

No-one had seen him at the airport either, but that didn't mean much. His ticket wouldn't have been pre-booked.

At this point in the conversation, I had to hang up. The phone may well be needed for Grace. I just couldn't cope anymore. I ran from the house to my place of refuge at the park in Glencoe.

Simm wasn't the only one who could be at a loss. I threw myself on the grass close to the lake and wept.

When I had no more tears to cry, I sat up and brooding, dangled my feet in the cool water, marring its mirrored surface with gravel.

I was still drawing the occasional labored breath when I saw Sunny across the pond. He wasn't looking at me. In fact, he was turned away. But from his demeanor, I could tell he wasn't happy. His shoulders were slumped, and he dragged his feet as if he was weary. My Sunny wasn't very sunny today. That was depressing in itself.

I couldn't shirk my responsibilities indefinitely.

I drove back to Grace's house and went to find Simm. He wasn't there but I found him walking in the garden. It was very cold and he was just in shirt-sleeves.

I took him indoors again and when his teeth began to chatter, found him a sweater, then made him some sweet hot chocolate. He sipped it slowly without enjoyment, but he did drink it. He'd yet to speak.

Was there anyone – anyone ever in the history of the world - who'd had to carry the weight I had at this moment? I wasn't sure how much longer I could do it. Everyone had baled on me.

I was feeling so sorry for myself. I think I'd have killed Grace for making my life so difficult – Gil too. Even Simm had failed me. Giulia had gone, God knew where, chasing my stupid father. Not even one guardian when I needed them most. Only the uncommunicative Sunny and even he'd turned away.

I couldn't go on like this. I stood, snatched Simm's chocolate out of his hand and drank it down. It scalded my throat and I coughed.

He looked up at me in surprise. At last a goddamn reaction. I was beginning to think he'd turned into a zombie.

"You're going to have to pull yourself together, Simm. I can't do all this on my own. Grace is seriously ill in hospital, my father has disappeared God knows where, Giulia is chasing after him. I can't even call Harry. No doubt he's out chasing stupid Gil as well. Snap out of it. You'll feel better if you're active."

He looked up at me with haunted eyes but at least they were focused again.

"Please forgive me. I've never felt so sorry for myself ever."

Oh, really? You don't say!

"I promise we will do this together from now on."

I sat on his knee, put my arms round his neck and whispered 'thank God' in his ear.

"Because if you hadn't said that I think I'd have hit you in the face with that frying pan."

He laughed for the first time in an age.

We took a hotel suite near the hospital when Grace was moved to Chicago and made sure one of us was always there to take any calls.

Simm, to his fury, was still working for his Dad and occasionally had to go to LA for business meetings so I spent some days alone.

It went without saying Oliver hadn't visited his mother once. Nor even, so far as I knew, asked after her.

With Grace we filled in where we were needed, showed her she was loved when she felt at her lowest, helped with a little initial physiotherapy, taking a Grace-sized slab of abuse when she got frustrated.

I said nothing to anyone but I could see it was hopeless. She was never going to live an independent life again. She knew it too.

The day came when they could do no more for her at the hospital and she was sent home to complete her recuperation.

We hired several home nurses but she behaved so appallingly to them that none of them lasted more than a few days.

During that time, she refused to be washed or do her exercises. She just sat in her wheelchair staring out at the garden. We didn't know if she could speak, she never tried. Just treated us as if she couldn't see us and rode by in her electric chariot.

I tried to fix her hair and apply a bit of makeup for her, thinking it might make her feel better. They were things she'd always prided herself on doing anyway. It broke my heart to see the perfectly coifed, silver hair she'd always been so particular about, now hanging in rat-tails about her shoulders.

Then one day she was gone. Extinguished like a candle flame. Poor Annie it was who again found her, cold and stiff in her chair. She ran to my room, face in her hands.

"Mrs. Maxwell's gone, Miss Christie. She's gone, she's gone!"

Annie was distraught and inconsolable.

I dragged her down the hall and told her in a whisper to control herself. I didn't want Simm to know until I'd assessed the situation for myself.

She led me to Grace's bedroom but hovered in the doorway while I looked for a non-existent pulse. Her skin was clammy but cold and her eyes half-open. Her patrician features were slewed to one side by the action of the stroke. My eyes filled with tears but I was glad for her it was all over.

Simm appeared at my shoulder. I thought he would be devastated but he just looked resigned.

He bent over me and took her hand to kiss it, but it wouldn't budge, but clasped in her frozen fingers was an old photograph, creased and crumpled from her iron grip. When we finally managed to extract it, it turned out to be of a tiny baby. On the rear in Grace's confident hand was written:

"Katrina Riviere de Beauvais, September 21st 1945"

"I guess that secret will go with her to the grave," said Simeon.

Chapter Three
Back to the End

Gil

I saw Harry, Bobby and David before I'd even got through the airport gate. They were clearly looking for someone. Probably me. I sneaked behind a couple of tall guys and managed to sidle past them and out of the sliding glass door.

The Westin was the closest available hotel, so I checked in.. A shower and change of clothes later, I was standing on the sidewalk, wondering what the hell to do to shift this rock in my stomach.

I'd dumped on the guys in the band – hadn't shown my face since Anaheim, walked out on Giulia and, by my actions, told my dearest friends they could go fuck themselves. Jamie and Connie were gone. I had a daughter who probably thought I'd lost my mind – which I had.

They mustn't find me in this state. It'd prove Connie right to have deserted me, even for a toad like Maxwell. How…how?

I couldn't do this alone and I'd left in such a panic I hadn't given it any thought.

The chain at my throat with the gold medallion was suddenly burning hot against my chest. Daniel…Daniel Jones. I'd go and see the Teacher. He'd always listened. I hadn't visited for such a long time.- would he remember me?

I took a cab to the Union of Souls headquarters. It was in a fairly affluent region of LA and resembled a European mansion house with arched windows on its extensive marble facade.

For a place of redemption it was about as far from the river Jordan as you could get.

Daniel's office had grown in opulence since the days when we three hippies – Harry, Daniel and I - would sit on a beat-up sofa in a booklined office, drinking tea with our feet up on a glass-topped coffee table.

In some respects, then it reminded me of my childhood home in Briarside and my Mom. Now the Movement had moved out of the city things had sure changed.

A secretary in pearls and a pencil skirt rapped politely on the solid oak door and showed me in.

Daniel was now a rounder, ruddier more affluent man than I remembered. He reminded me of Pastor Frank at our local church when I was a choir boy.

"Gil…. Come in, come in… delighted to see you. The years have treated you well."

Bull-shit. This was not looking good.

"What can I do for you, my son."

Sounded like Pastor Frank as well.

"I didn't know where else to go, Daniel. Can you help me? I need somewhere to stay for a few days until I can get myself together."

"A little meditation might be the answer, don't you

think? Put you back in touch with your soul. Naturally you can stay."

I sighed with relief and felt myself relaxing. Someone understood, someone with no ax to grind.

"I'm so grateful, Daniel. Just a few days would be great. Then I'll explain the whole damn mess to you. Thank you."

He called his secretary on the intercom and took a key down from a rack on the wall – a bit like a hotel desk.

"Linda, show my friend to room 402. I'll drop by later, Gil. Make yourself at home. You should find everything you need there."

The room was comfortably but sparsely furnished. There was a single bed and nightstand with a lamp, a chest of drawers with an ivory candle holder and candle, and a prie dieu in one corner with a china jar of sandalwood incense sticks on the top. The Union of Souls symbol, like the one on my medallion, hung on the wall above.

I'd left all my belongings at the Westin but found a couple of meditation robes in one of the dresser drawers.

I lit a candle and with great difficulty – shit, it was an eternity since I'd done this – I managed to kneel on the prayer mat, close my eyes and take a deep breath to center myself.

The candle flame, with its faint blue aura flickered momentarily until I had control of my breathing. I stared into its peaceful heart.

No rose water – no Connie. My eyes snapped open – perhaps I needed to rest a little first. Nerves were disturbing my concentration.

I blew out the candle and lay on the bed watching the ribbon of blue smoke rise into the air.

Then I must have slept because the room was darkening when I was woken by an authoritative rap at the door.

Daniel stood in the doorway holding a tray on which was food and a glass of water.

"How are you managing? Got everything you need? I thought you might appreciate a bite to eat"

He placed the tray on top of the chest of drawers and sat next to me on the bed. I thanked him for his thoughtfulness.

He put his hand on my arm and looked at me seriously:

"Of course I want you to stay, my friend, as long as you want or need but…"

Oh shit!

"I've just had a phone call from our leader in San Francisco and we've a lecture weekend to organize beginning Friday. There's already a meditation seminar planned for the same time. We won't have accommodation for you after tomorrow night. That will have given you three days – that should be enough, shouldn't it?"

So much for stay as long as you like. The days of the soul, it seemed, had given way to a fast buck.

I wept with despair, and Daniel left in embarrassment.

I didn't see him again. The occasional tray of food appeared at the door. I'd tried and tried to meditate my way to some kind of calm but Connie and Christie's – and occasionally Giulia's and my Mom's - faces haunted my mind, so in the end I gave up and left.

I was disillusioned to the point of embarrassment. I'd put my trust in the wrong person yet again, but far worse, I had begun to doubt the Spirit which had been my mainstay for an entire lifetime. I could never speak of this again, especially to Harry.

I went to Rick's. Where else was there to go alone in Los Angeles at night, a stranger in a city I'd called home for so many years.

Ricks looked smaller and more run-down than I remembered. I stood across the street and observed the place where my life had ended.

Even in my present state of mind I knew I was being so heartlessly unkind to Giulia. I put that to one side for the minute. I couldn't take any more problems on board yet.

I didn't know if I was relieved to see Pete behind the bar or not. He looked so much older. I guessed I must have too. That Christmas Day so long ago, when he'd hoisted me drunk and incapable into his car and driven me home, seemed only yesterday, but was before Connie had left.

He slapped a Bud and a shot of Jim Beam on the counter. My God, things must have been bad if he could remember my poison all these years on. I paid him. Not a word was exchanged.

The upholstery was new but the seating was the same. I slid into my habitual booth, intending to get well and truly inebriated. I could think of no other way to anesthetize the overwhelming depression coursing through my body. Maybe if I could get blind drunk it might recede, at least for a while.

But naturally, when you need alcohol the most, it does the least. Perhaps it was as well. Getting locked up by the police would only add to my troubles.

I wandered down to Venice. The beach that Jamie loved so much was now a hotch-potch of peeling paint and market-stalls. Not a surfboard in sight. None of the beautiful beach-babes Jamie had lusted after.

Santa Monica pier where he and I had fished for hours on end to escape a beating from our Dad, was empty and silent. It was here Giulia had saved me from myself when Connie's loss was killing me.

Now that she and Oliver were winding up, I had hoped there might be a chance for us to try again. As soon as I had the thought I dismissed it. Never in a million years could I do that to Giulia.

I don't know why she loved me so much. Usually, I loved her for her kindness but tonight it felt like a noose.

Chapter Four

The Posse Assembles

Christie

There was no autopsy. Grace had died at home with those she loved and trusted.

Connie arrived the following day. Despite their occasional disagreements, there was a real bond of friendship between Connie and Grace. Afterall, they had a common enemy!

We found an address book in her desk drawer and went through it, letting her acquaintances know she'd passed away. There didn't appear to have been any relatives but those in Los Angeles.

Simm called his Dad and asked that he come and bring Deborah. Oliver said he'd some business to transact and he'd call back. He never did. Simm looked so disappointed. If I'd had a gun I'd have gone to LA and shot the bastard myself.

I told him not to mind – Connie was better and anyway he'd just have to make do with me instead.

I was gratified to see he cheered up instantly.

The funeral was not well attended. She pretty much held the human race in contempt. We were her few exceptions.

I called my Mom and Dad in Champaign and asked if

they'd like to be there, but they sent some beautiful flowers instead.

Simm and I commissioned an elegant marble tomb for her, carved with her name and the names of her grandson and honorary granddaughter. We didn't bother with Oliver or Deborah. They probably would never see it anyway. I still didn't know why she'd hated him so much.

It wasn't until after the funeral I had a chance to sit down and chat to Connie. After we had reminisced about Grace and laughed at her idiosyncrasies, I tackled the problem of Gil.

I told her of his surprise arrival at Windham and his reaction. With all that had been happening, I'd completely forgotten to call her.

"He bolted - Giulia thought perhaps it was because I looked so exactly like you when you were my age and it shocked him."

"It's probably your hair – you saw the photo of our wedding day. Gil was mortified when I cut it off - I did it on a whim without telling him. He spent the rest of the day doused in candle wax at the pool-house."

She laughed, then was immediately sorry.

"I'll leave Simm here." I said, "There's the reading of Grace's Will and her business affairs to wind up. I think he'll be okay with that. It's been a week now. would you help me find Gil? He's not in Colorado so my best guess is LA. Can I come back with you?"

"Are you sure you want to get into this? Gil loves his

music, and apart from the people who appreciate it, it's all he truly loves. You may find him and it maybe he is so preoccupied he has no time for you. That's the root of what happened with me and his sons."

It still hurt, I could easily see.

"It's a gene I seem to have inherited," I said. "I love my piano so much when I'm playing I think of nothing else. You know that's true – you've seen it. Do you know where we can start?"

"If this is rooted in the past I have one or two ideas. If not, Giulia will know. But either way, we have no time to lose – a week is a long time in this situation."

"Giulia has no idea where he's' gone. She's been looking for days and hasn't found him."

Chapter Five

Search for an Absent Brother

Gil

Perhaps if I could talk to Mom – explain - there might be a shred of comfort there. But the house was dark. Not a glimmer of light or a sign of life anywhere.

I felt dizzy and had to lean against the gatepost for a few moments to regain my balance. Perhaps I wasn't as sober as I thought.

I took a cab downtown again and I walked the streets, past old haunts and familiar apartment blocks. I wondered if anyone I'd known was still around. But it was twenty years ago – they'd all have moved on.

I passed a cellar club I'd once played at. The light beckoned me.

The owner, who was serving behind the bar told me he hadn't been able to book an act for that night, and when I asked if I could play he directed me over to a decrepit old piano on a raised platform.

I should have thought of this before - I would drown myself in music.

It worked for a while, but then my situation hit me again, and I put down the piano lid and rested my head in my hands. There was a spattering of applause from the meagre crowd.

As I stood to leave, the owner shoved something into my hand although I hadn't asked for payment.

"Here, pal. You look as if you could use this."

He'd given me a few milligrams of cocaine as payment.

I should have thrown it away, but I didn't. Instead it made me think of Jamie, always high as a kite. The pain in my chest came back worse than ever as I tucked the cocaine into the pocket of my jeans.

I called in at a couple of bars on my way, but the booze was making me maudlin. I leaned against the cold concrete wall outside an apartment block for a few minutes until I was sure I could stand upright unaided. The alcohol seemed to have affected my legs but not my brain.

I couldn't get Jamie out of my mind. For the first time since the moment on the mountain where he'd committed me to the care of Harry and David, I felt close to him. I'd go and see him.

The cemetery was only a mile down the road from where I stood. Perhaps I could walk off the despair and share a few minutes with him. He'd talked to me when I'd needed him before – perhaps he would again.

And Christie? I'd die before I subjected her to what had driven Connie and the boys away. For the first time I really understood why Connie and Giulia had joined forces. It may be I'd never know my daughter at all.

I staggered on.

At the gates of the cemetery I stood for a few

moments unsure what to do. What would I do if his grave was choked with weeds, the headstone illegible?

But I'd come this far so I took a deep breath and walked in.

The gravel paths were as well-kept as I remembered, the grass neatly mown. Jamie's grave had been visible from the gate but it was pitch dark, and the cemetery had no lighting.

Still I found it without much difficulty.

I needn't have been concerned. I'd reckoned without my mother. The grave was cleared and a bunch of fresh yellow roses placed where his head must be laid. Here and there across the grave were placed single red roses and a couple of small bouquets, all the worse for wear. Twenty years on and fans were still leaving him gifts. I picked them up and dropped them in a nearby waste bin.

I thought of his laughter, his thick, sun-streaked hair and the love in his eyes for the whole world. When he left, a huge chunk of me went with him.

I ran my fingers along the headstone as Connie and I had done the day after his funeral. Connie.

Chapter Six

Beginning of the Trail

Christie

When everyone had gone and Connie and I had the opportunity to consider our options, we decided the best course of action was to sit down and make a list as detailed as possible of where Gil might have gone, that may or may not have been at the bottom of the Pacific Ocean.

I winced. I was so glad that thought hadn't found its way out of my mouth when I remembered what had happened to Jamie.

The list included some of his favorite recording studios, a couple of bars he frequented with special mention of Rick's on Sunset, Pandora's Box nightclub, his mother's house, but definitely not his father's, Venice where Jamie once lived, Santa Monica pier where he and Jamie had so often fished.

As an after-thought she added Jamie's grave, but she didn't think he'd go there for other, private reasons. She must have forgotten she'd spilled the beans at Grace's house in front of a whole room full of people.

There were other places – Connie and Gil's former home. That had been redeveloped a decade ago, but she supposed he might have gone there out of sentiment.

She slipped the paper and ball-point in her purse, saying she'd give it some more thought on the plane home.

As it turned out, I couldn't accompany Connie to Los Angeles straight away. Simm had been named as Grace's Personal Representative, and he wanted me to go with him to register the Will with the Probate Office before I left.

I asked Connie to go on ahead and I'd follow as quickly as I could, hopefully the following day.

Son-of-a-bitch, I'd kill him if he'd committed suicide before I'd had a chance to get to know him. Logic under stress was never my strong suit.

Simm ran me to the airport from the County Probate office in Chicago and I arrived in LA at around six. Connie met me at the gate and we drove straight to her Santa Monica apartment.

By California standards it was quite small and consisted of, in addition to the comfortable living room, three reasonably sized bedrooms, a dining kitchen and a luxurious bathroom. There was a parking garage and storage unit beneath.

It was spick and span as could be expected of Connie who was an exceptionally neat and tidy person.

If you opened the window fully you could hear the ocean at the bottom of the street.

"Did you get time to go through the list?" I asked.

"A little. I checked out the studios but got absolutely no help at all."

"Did you expect to?"

"Not really although Gil was very well-known and well-liked. But he was Jamie's brother and Jamie had caused so much trouble at practically every studio in Los Angeles, that Gil had been tarred with the same brush. In the end, they turned out to be right – Gil became almost as much trouble as Jamie.

"They were polite but not helpful. The people who did want to help had known Gil as a boy. They were getting on and hadn't heard from him in years.

The paper before her had a few items crossed off the top in red pen.

"Where do you suggest we try next?"

"I think perhaps Rick's Bar. It was always where he went to get wasted when we were having problems." Oh God, poor Gil! "It's also where we went, the four of us, to arrange our separations. It was a devastating meeting for both of us."

We checked it out.

The barman said he'd been in the day before and he was surprised because he hadn't seen him in years. Gil was still drinking beer with bourbon chasers, so he hadn't changed that much.

Another bit of information I could have done without. I took a step behind Connie's shoulder. This was getting scary.

"Had he much to drink?"

"Oh yes, but he still walked out more or less in a straight line. I've seen him worse."

Connie looked worried. Apparently, Gil drinking a lot then walking in a straight line was not necessarily a good thing. She handed the barman a card.

"If you see him again, please will you call this number?"

"Surely." He placed the card on top of a pile of similar cards next to the cash register.

Chapter Seven

The Old Poison

Gil

I sat stock-still on the very same bench Connie and I had shared all those years ago. It was new then. Now the paint was cracked in places and the wood showing through.

I gripped in my hand the crystal the monk in the mountain retreat had given me so long ago, but it appeared to have lost its power. Its color had faded over time so perhaps its strength had dissipated with it, since it had no effect.

I stared at the grave until a misty dawn broke on the eastern horizon.

All that time, I had been willing Jamie to talk to me, but he didn't. The air was cold and empty. It held no trace of the loving spirit which had kept me afloat so many times. How had I survived twenty years without him? Only Connie, who had been there could understand. Only Connie.

I was cold and stiff from the inactivity. I stood and stretched. No point in staying here - it was as sterile as the rest of my life.

At the nearest all-night drug store I bought a bottle of vodka. Might as well salute him with his own poison.

I sat on the ground in the store's parking lot, my back

to the building wall. A quarter of the bottle went down my throat in one swallow. In my increasingly addled mind I would picture Jamie….. with his arm around Connie. No. It wasn't Connie. Fuck! It was Christie. I'd jerked upright at the image but relaxed back against the wall. Perhaps I'd died of alcohol poisoning. Who would care?

I was vaguely aware of a bunch of school kids who had stopped to stare at me. I pulled a face at them, lost balance and flopped sideways onto the ground where I fell into a stupor, clutching the bottle to my chest like a teddy bear.

I must have stayed like that for at least an hour because when I came to, cars were beginning to turn into the lot. I needed to leave.

I don't know if I'd intended to go back to the cemetery or not. I can't remember. But that's where I ended up.

Through the gate, I sat under some overhanging trees and took another swig. - until I realized which tree I'd chosen to sit beneath. Would you fucking believe it? All the trees in the freakin' world I could sit under, and it had to be this one.

I went back to Jamie's bench. I hadn't felt this bad since Connie first left me.

Connie, Christie, Jamie. They'd all gone. But Christie hadn't – at least not knowingly and not by choice. But all those I loved and relied on left me eventually. It was only a matter of time before she took the same road.

Only the music remained. Only my friends understood.

I didn't seem able to get off this helter-skelter. I was sinking faster and faster, lower and lower. What would happen when I reached the bottom?

But there was a way out, at least temporarily and Jamie had shown me how all those years ago. My brother would understand.

It felt like an electric shock so strong I looked about for its cause. But the burial ground looked deserted and serenely peaceful. Besides, I was too distracted to care.

I took the little plastic envelope the club owner had given me and looked at it. Again, the jolt, This time it seemed to shake the headstone. I put it down to the booze.

I knew the consequences of taking the coke. I'd suffered through them twice already. But surely one dose could only help. I'd share this one last snort with Jamie.

I lined the cocaine up on the top of his gravestone, took a note from my billfold and sniffed as deeply as I could.

The high was immediate. I steadied myself against the stone and felt the warmth spread through my body and my mood begin to lighten. From waning, my heart rate went through the roof.

Then there was a sharp pain in my head and the whole world descended into blackness. My last, shuddering thought wasn't Connie, but Christie.

Chapter Eight
Lost

Christie

We checked Pandora's. It was locked and shuttered and no amount of banging on the door could raise an answer.

Our final option was to drive down to Venice.

It was such a seedy area, Connie refused point-blank to let me out of the car. Why would Gil choose to come here?

Connie said this is where Jamie had slept rough at his lowest point. Gil spent countless nights trawling the streets for him. There was a slim chance he might be there. We didn't see him, although Connie drove round and round.

At one intersection while we were stopped, a very dubious character banged violently on the roof of the car. Connie took off down the road against the lights.

We cruised slowly down the ocean front as close as we could get to the beach. Despite Connie's nervousness we even got out of the car for a while to check out the beach-side walk. Nothing.

She drove past the street she lived on and ended up at Santa Monica pier. Nothing.

"We won't find him now" said Connie. Let's go back to my place, get some sleep and start again in the morning."

The sky was paling to silver-grey over the city as she spoke. The morning was almost here.

I fell into bed exhausted and scared. My body unwound but my brain was racing. I couldn't stop it. I felt cold and terrified and had a storming headache. I'd never suffered from migraine in my life but guessed this is how it must have felt.

I took a shower which helped a bit.

The door buzzer sounded and I went to answer it but Connie in her robe was there before me.

On the doorstep stood my guardians minus Deedee but with David. Giulia, looking unspeakably embarrassed, was standing on the other side of the alleyway behind them.

Connie waved them inside, and when Giulia didn't move she took her by the arm and said encouragingly:

"This time we have a common cause. It would be a waste of time and effort to fight each other. Come on inside - we haven't had breakfast yet."

"Thank you. That's very kind," said Giulia with a wan smile.

It was only seven in the morning. That we'd only had three hours sleep was apparent. But the others didn't look a lot better. Harry kept taking off his glasses, rubbing his eyes and putting them back on. David's head was resting on an arm which kept collapsing sideways and jerking him awake again. Only Bobby looked fully conscious. Other than being the color of parchment he was at least capable of coherent speech.

"We've been to all his old hangouts" reported Connie. "The only place they recognized him was Rick's where he'd had a skinful then disappeared into the night."

"Forgot about Ricks." said Giulia, shamefaced. "I shouldn't have. He used to drink there with my brother Larry."

Giulia didn't mention her brother often. He'd been her favorite but he'd died when she was still in her teens.

"He wasn't there," said Connie, "but I left a card with the barman. He remembered him from twenty years ago. He'd good cause."

She looked down at her hands folded on the table and I took one of them between my own. She smiled her thanks.

"Right, breakfast?" she said.

There were relieved nods all round and I went to give her a hand.

Halfway through making it, her head suddenly snapped up and as she ran to get her jacket, she yelled over her shoulder:

"Goddamn – I know where he is! Why didn't I think of it before? He wouldn't have gone to the grave for Jamie, but Christie is another matter!"

She shot out of the door, down the steps and jumped in her car, keying it to life. I only just managed to get in before she raced down the street at top speed.

Giulia's car had been left behind but fortunately the streets hadn't come to early morning life yet, so she was able to catch up.

We roared through the city. Any cop intent on giving her a ticket would have been wasting his time. I glanced at Giulia behind us, grimly hanging onto the steering wheel with a decidedly nervous Bobby beside her. He'd one hand braced against the roof.

Connie screeched to a halt in front of the cemetery gates where Jamie was interred, and yelled at me:

"He wouldn't come here for Jamie but he would come for you," she said decisively.

When I looked up again, I was pleased to see Sunny smiling encouragingly at me from beside the gatepost. He beckoned me to follow him.

Giulia's car drew up behind Connie's. The rest of them tumbled out, in a state of shock. You could read 'shit, we survived' written clearly on every face.

"Sunny says he's this way," I said, indicating the gates. I almost missed the look of consternation which passed between them. But not quite.

"Oh. He's not there now - he walked on ahead."

"Never mind that," snapped Connie, bolting for the gates.

We followed in hot pursuit until Connie stopped dead in her tracks and threw out both arms to stop us.

Gil was half-propped against Jamie's grave, mouth open, eyes half shut and with a long jagged cut on his forehead which had leaked blood, now dry, down the side of his face to tangle with his beard and drip on his shoulder. He was so devoid of color he looked dead.

Before Connie could move, Giulia ran forward and lifted his wrist to feel for a pulse.

"He's alive," she said. "But his pulse is racing. We need to get him to a hospital. I can't take him home like this."

Gil's left hand shot out and grabbed her hard by the wrist.

"No. NO! Santa Monica," he groaned and lost consciousness again.

"Is there a hospital in Santa Monica?" asked Giulia. Connie shook her head.

The three men carried Gil to Giulia's car and laid him on the back seat. By this time, he'd begun to regain consciousness. His right wrist stuck out at an odd angle, and he screamed with pain every time it was moved.

Connie held me tightly to her when I wanted to go and help. She shook her head.

"You can't help. Leave them to it."

"We ought to take him to hospital" said Bobby, worried. "That head wound looks pretty bad. There could be other injuries we can't see."

"His wrist's broken," said David laconically. "He's wasted and stoned."

"Oh my God, not again," gasped Connie. "No, please

not again. Giulia, believe me, you don't want this."

Giulia bit her lip and looked distraught – she'd once had to deal with him in a similar condition, but of that Connie was unaware.

"Please don't worry," I said with a great deal of sympathy. "We'll do whatever we can for him. You just tell us what."

"And he's been rolled," added Harry, checking Gil's clothes. "His billfold's gone. A mugging would account for the head wound."

"This must be a renowned spot for it." said Connie.

"He's still yours Connie. Even now he wants to go home with you. Not to Colorado where we've lived all these years." Giulia sobbed into her hands. "How will I ever get used to it."

"We can't hang about here with him in this state while you two discuss your love lives," I snapped, my nerves making me cranky.

Chapter Nine
Full Circle Comedy

Christie

Gil gradually regained consciousness as we motored home. I drove Giulia's car – she wasn't able – she was shaking like a leaf.

The vodka and cocaine had left him groggy and disco-ordinated.

Harry sat with his head raised on his lap and kept checking his pupils. His arm he held clasped over his chest to keep it still. The rest of the guys were with Connie.

Over and over Gil moaned "Santa Monica, Santa Monica."

At times he became so distressed Harry had to hold him down. Hospital, clearly, was not an option.

Giulia was sobbing into her sleeve. She couldn't understand how he could have deserted her so utterly. When she looked at me there was pleading in her expression, but for what I didn't know.

We arrived at Connie's apartment. The guys half-walked, half-carried Gil up the steps, trying to ignore his screams of pain.

I had them lay him on my bed while Connie went to call her doctor.

Several times the agitation caused by the cocaine

made him try to rise, only to sink down again in agony.

The doctor came and shouted at us. Why the hell wasn't he in hospital?

At last, David had had more than he could take.

"Because he fucking won't go, you moron! Do we look deluded to you?"

The doctor, not a young man, had clearly seen it all before, so he ignored the outburst.

Connie was asked to find two pieces of wood to make a splint. She had David break the back off a wooden kitchen chair and remove two of the spokes.

The doctor pulled Gil's broken wrist into line and used them as splints. Gil passed out halfway through. The doc gave him a shot of pain killer. Gil came round.

Next, the doctor felt his forehead and checked his eyes with a torch before throwing it back in his bag in frustration. He cleaned and dressed the head wound.

"I hate people like this." *Nice – very professional*. "After cocaine and alcohol how am I supposed to check for brain damage?"

"We'll give you another call if he gets worse," said David.

"How will you know he's worse?" came back the doctor, irritated.

He snapped his bag shut and made for the door.

"My account will be in the post Mrs. Maxwell."

The Twinkle in Pa's Eye

Thanks to the effects of the cocaine, Gil wasn't yet completely lucid, but he was a thousand per cent better than he'd been when we found him.

We managed to strip off his dirty clothes, while he kept reaching out to me and calling me Connie, then he would call Connie, Christie. About one in ten he hit it right.

Giulia sent us all out and bathed him head to toe. I thought that was a bit prim for a band member's wife, but I had no particular desire to see my father in the nude. Connie tutted. Presumably because she'd seen it all before. I wondered if she was curious if he'd changed – physically, I meant. I would have been overwhelmed with curiosity. Not Connie. Water under the bridge, I supposed.

The doctor had sent a nurse to set his arm since Gil still refused point blank to move to a hospital, saying once he went in, the only way he'd get out was in a straight-jacket.

He may not have been wrong. I was having serious doubts of his sanity and was hoping it wasn't genetic. I took it to be rock star histrionics. Too much money, too little knowledge of how to use it.

All three of the other guys lived in LA, so when they'd left for home, Connie, Giulia and I rested, too wound up to sleep properly.

I was so proud of my mother and stepmother. How many other people in their situation would have behaved in such a civilized manner?

Connie said to me:

"Don't think it's always been this way. We have

always been jealous of each other, but we've had to put that aside – for the time being at least. The real test will come when…" Connie rolled her eyes. "…. *if* this is all over.

"You asked me a question, Christie, and Giulia will feel better for knowing too. The reason Gil was so desperate to get here was that…" she pointed at my bedroom door, "Christie was born in that room."

That made me shiver. Then I grinned. Connie understood the look on my face and we both burst out laughing at the ridiculousness of Gil laying in the very same bed where I first saw the light of day.

But Giulia, who had missed the point, was aghast.

"I assumed she'd been born at the Maxwell house in Bel Air. Gil did too. Why?"

"Oliver wouldn't hear of it. This was my mother's apartment. As soon as Christie was born, my mother registered her birth in California. You were registered as Anna Robson Maxwell. First name for my grandmother, second for your father and the last for Grace – not the idiot I lived with. Then you were whipped off to Illinois to stay with Grace so Gil wouldn't find you. Grace found foster parents for you."

Foster parents? Until six months ago I'd thought they were my birth parents. Was nothing as it seemed?

Turning back to Giulia she said:

"Her birth was registered here to distract him. I dreaded him moving heaven and earth to find you," she said to me. "Fortunately, Jacob and Mylo were saved by a fantastic grandmother in Nancy Robson, who took them in. By the time Gil and I formally separated, neither wanted to leave her. It was a just punishment."

She looked thoughtful for a moment then sighed.

"My problem with Gil has always been one of communication. He sometimes exists on another plane from the rest of us – I know, odd, isn't it? He's unreachable for anyone else except complete strangers. He somehow seems to recognize it in his friends, his audiences. From babies to the elderly, they seem to get him in a way I never could."

The germ of an idea began to form in my mind. Perhaps all was not lost. But first I must get to know him and that might not be so easy.

Gil was clearly feeling better. He began to shout out for food and some clothes so he could get out of bed.

"Fuck that!" said Connie, at the top of her voice.

It always knocked me for six that such a well-spoken lady could come out with that word.

"Stay there. Giulia will bring you some food. If I fetch it, it'll end up over your head, you selfish bastard!"

Silence.

"I'm going to bed. Feel free," she said indicating the kitchen.

"He's not going anywhere," said Giulia with a crafty grin. "We cut the clothes off him, and he doesn't have any more."

Chapter Ten

Guardians Past and Present

Christie

Connie called Harry and asked him to go to the Airport Westin and pick up Gil's belongings.

"They won't give them to me," said Harry. "Firstly, I'm not Gil and secondly, you can ask him but I'd like to bet his key-card was in his billfold which was stolen."

I snatched the phone from his hand.

"It doesn't matter." I said, "I'll have Gil write a signed note of authorization. He can explain the predicament himself."

"You mean cocaine, alcohol and lack of pants?" said Harry wryly. "Wish I was there."

Even Giulia, who was mostly serious when it came to Gil, had to smile.

"Oh, please let me ask him!" said Connie.

It was amazing how cavalier they were now there was no chance of him dying on them. The poor guy must have been so confused.

"I'll come with you," said Giulia. Make that double confused.

"I think I'd better bring the note down myself." I said, maintaining my cool with difficulty. "Meet you in the foyer in a couple of hours."

Confused was a mild description of what Gil was.

His wife and ex-wife were sitting one on either side of his bed, and neither could speak long enough to explain what they wanted. I hung back in the doorway and watched.

In the end I snatched the paper and pen from Connie's hand and explained that if he wanted to get out of bed, he'd need pants which he didn't have – or anything else either, come to that. So, if he wanted to fix that, he'd better write a note of explanation to the hotel so Harry could pick up his stuff.

My God, he was handsome, even in his forties with a black eye.

He wrote the note and handed me back the paper. As he did so he let both note and pen fall on the bed and grasped my hand, massaging it between his own. There were tears in his soft blue eyes and he was silently pleading with me for…something. Shit, I wished I was better at this!

Reluctantly, he released my hand, letting our fingers slip apart.

I picked up the note and folded it. Both Connie and Giulia were looking at me speculatively.

"Please come back," he whispered. How could I not? Perhaps he'd need rescuing from his wives.

I met Harry in the foyer of the Westin as arranged. David was with him.

"How'd it go?" asked David.

"You know him, so I would guess about as well as you'd expect."

He rubbed his hands and grinned.

"Come on, you guys, let's get the stuff and get to Connie's"

He took the note I proffered, scanned it quickly and took it to the desk clerk.

"Oh, don't rush." I said, "He's in good hands."

Probably.

Harry and David accompanied a bellhop to pick up Gil's belongings so I wandered into the hotel coffee shop.

It was a full half hour before they reappeared. Harry was carrying Gil's leather sports bag.

"Man," said Davy. "You never saw anything like that room. It must have taken some energy to get it in that state."

"He'd stopped short of tossing the TV out of the window. It was nailed shut," added Harry. "Sorry – only joking – Crystal Band not some sixties deadhead."

I laughed at their teasing but worried there might be some truth in it – after all they were all a children of the sixties themselves.

"Come on, Christie. No way can this be your fault. Let's go see him and put your mind at rest."

I fingered my medallion thoughtfully.

"Sit a minute longer. Tell me more about these."

"We all belong to a spiritualist church," said Harry. "Our jobs are loud and sometimes overpowering so we often need a way to unwind. For a long time Gil was led down the path of recreational drugs – mostly by Jamie – when life got too much for him. And when he lost Connie, he was completely adrift. We'd seen too much of the substance scene to get involved. There were heartbreaking deaths in both our bands."

"Gil has had a crap life," said David, suddenly serious.

"Yes, Connie told me," I replied

"They took all he gave then demanded more. From his teens he was dumped on by everyone, especially those he loved best.

"Harry joined this particular movement years ago and gradually brainwashed the rest of us into it."

Harry smiled:

"We all wear the medallion. When they were still married, Gil gave one to Connie as a love token."

"This is it - the one I'm wearing. I always knew it was very special to her."

"You'll grasp then, what it meant to him."

I twisted its delicate form between my fingers.

"I'll never take it off. Not unless either Gil or Connie tell me to."

"Gil had a natural leaning towards spirituality. He never needed to learn," Harry continued thoughtfully as if I hadn't spoken. "I have worked hard for enlightenment most of my life without getting there. It's part of Gil's make up. He never even has to try.

"For example, candle-light is an aid to meditation in most religions. Gil viewed even the smallest candle flame as the center of the universe. Most adherents use joss sticks and essential oils with it, but Gil only used the scent of roses and scattered rosewater. He's done both without thinking as long as I've known him. But such is the weight he's carried all these years, in the end even this has failed him.

"Ed Morris – also in the 'Crystal Band' - is a prime example of what meditation is not….. "

"Yes, we've met, if you remember." I said with loathing.

"He's riddled with jealousy. Gil is a superbly gifted musician with an unmatched voice. He is, without effort, what Ed would like to be and never will achieve. He hates him for it. He's another weight Gil has had to carry."

"Stop!" I ordered. "No more. How can this paragon have produced me?"

They looked at each other and laughed.

"Oh, he's no paragon," said David. "The son-of-a-bitch has one hell of a temper. Ask the sidemen!"

"And here comes one of them now! Hope you don't mind," he said to me. "He wanted to make sure Gil was good," and louder. "Afterall, he hero-worships your Dad. Bobby'd kiss his feet if Gil would let him."

He turned to me again:

"And talking of feet - that's another thing that makes

him human. Truly, we've spent a lifetime trying to talk him out of those white socks."

Bobby flicked his ear as he walked past, turned a chair and sat astride it.

"How's it going guys…and gal. And don't fill her head with that garbage. She'll believe you."

"Now why would she do that?" beamed David.

Harry looked at me over his glasses.

"This guy's about the best all-rounder in the business," he said, gesturing towards Bobby. "Excepting Gil who beats us all. Our bands have some of the world's best-selling albums, but Gil leaves us standing for musicianship."

"I've heard a number of different versions of why I was being stalked," I said, using the word to provoke a response. "What's yours?"

"Mostly it was to keep you safe. Ed isn't the only bastard in Gil's life. Being the best at what you do makes enemies.

"You were also our ace. If Gil lost it again, he might give it one last try for you. One day he may not want to come back to us, Christie. Grace knew about us and gave us her blessing," said Harry. "And if Grace knew I'd put money on Connie knowing too."

And here was me thinking *I* was keeping it from *them*. I wondered in passing if the shouting match in the sitting-room at Windham hadn't had something to do with this. Perhaps Oliver was 'him' and 'that bastard', both expressions frequently used by Grace to describe her son.

"They did? Son of a bitch!" There were a few extra titbits amongst that little lot.

"That's the way it began but as time when on, we began to find you…. interesting." said Bobby, who arrived balancing a tray of Cappuccinos. "For one thing you could knock hell out of a piano. Gil is going to love that. And you were very quick picking up a different style. That's a real Robson trait. Gil has it in spades. Jamie could have been the best of all but he squandered his talent."

All three where quiet, ruminating on their own memories.

"We'll go down to Santa Monica but first I'd like to drop by my place and pick up a guitar. It'll give him something to think about other than his own troubles. Why don't you and Bobby take his bag and we'll meet you there?" said Harry.

By the time we arrived, things were really kicking off.

Gil had finally lost his temper about being stuck in bed. He was sitting on the sofa, wrapped in the bedcover and trying to eat a cheese sandwich covered in mayonnaise. Every time he picked up the sandwich, the bedcover slid down his chest. Giulia tried to help but all Connie could do was laugh. She must have been one hell of a wife.

So, oh boy, was he pleased to see us! Connie stopped laughing when he slapped the sandwich with mayonnaise, down on her white sofa and it slipped off the plate.

He grabbed the bag and made a dash for the bathroom, the cover trailed behind him on the floor leaving a rare view of bare butt as he dashed through the door.

"Very dignified," I observed.

Connie got some stain remover from the kitchen.

Bobby was laughing fit to burst.

Twenty minutes later, dignity restored, Gil emerged from the bathroom showered, beard trimmed and smelling of Connie's shower gel.

"Sorry," he glowered at her. "There's hair in your sink."

Chapter Eleven
Simm Remembered

Christie

As good luck would have it, Harry and David turned up, just in time to see Connie glower back.

"Goddamn," grinned Davy. "Just like the old days."

"The hell it is" rejoined Connie. "We only have to deal with each other part time now. Giulia's got that privilege."

But there was sadness in the eyes of both of them. And Giulia's too.

'How can people go on living like this for a lifetime?' I thought. 'Can't live with each other, can't live without. And sweet loving Giulia stuck between them.'

It would be best if Gil and Connie moved away from each other. But then I saw they couldn't. Just couldn't. I wasn't sure I wanted to get in the middle of this tangle.

And that put me in mind of…Simm! I'd given him not one thought while all this had been happening and I'd left him to deal with Grace's estate alone.

"Can I use the phone in your room, Connie? I need to call Simm. I've left him with all Grace's affairs to deal with on his own. While I was out chasing you," I said to Gil, pointedly.

"Who's Simm?" asked Gil

"Connie's stepson and my boyfriend."

"What?" said everyone in the room except Connie.

"How did that get past us?" asked Harry, amazed.

"Oh, there was a lot got past you. You didn't know about Ed until it was too late. Then it was Sunny who found me."

"Who the hell is Sunny?" demanded Gil, head swiveling in confusion.

"Figment of her imagination," said David.

"Phone, Connie."

"Sure, go ahead"

I dialed Grace's number but Simm wasn't there. I knew there was no hope in hell of him being with his Dad and Deborah so I called the house in San Clemente.

"Yeah?" said a voice on the other end of the line. "Simeon Maxwell."

"It's me, Simm." I said.

"Whose me? Do I know you?"

"Don't be like that, Simm. You've no idea of the mayhem here. Everybody'd lost Gil. We couldn't find him anywhere. Thanks to Connie, we found him collapsed and unconscious next to Jamie's grave. Since then, we've been trying to sort him out. But for that, I'd have rung long ago. Why don't you come up here or would you rather I came to San Clemente?"

Simm sighed and I knew instantly his anger had melted.

"Who's we?"

"Connie and Giulia, Harry Forster, David Elliot and your uncle Bobby."

"Wow, and with all those you still couldn't find him? Substance abuse I take it. I've known him a long time, Christie."

"There's a chance it isn't going to stop any time soon either. It's the saddest situation. Please come - I need your help," I begged. "I'm going to need to speak to Gil alone at some point. He's depressed as hell at the moment - cocaine I guess - but I'm praying it won't be more than a one-off. He's surrounded by more support than he can cope with. Its driving him mad."

Simm laughed out loud.

"I can imagine with Connie and Giulia in the same room vying over him. I bet he wishes he was on another planet."

"Surprisingly, looking out for him seems to have brought them together."

"I never ever thought I'd say this, but nobody deserves that kind of grief."

"Huge change of subject. You remember how what I said embarrassed us both just before I left? Ssshh, it was true then – and just as true now. I hope you can cope with that."

Too long a silence.

"I'll be there in the morning."

He put the phone down.

When I went to join the others, a harassed Gil was taking the guitar and had begun to strum.

"It's tuned wrong," he told Harry in a grumpy tone of voice. "I can't play on this."

"Ungrateful bastard," said David on Harry's behalf.

"It's not tuned at all. I replaced a couple of strings – then looking for you intervened," said Harry.

Gil humphed and proceeded to tune the guitar.

Harry's supposition was correct. The guitar took Gil's entire attention.

He didn't even notice when I came and sat on the floor near his feet. Or at least, I didn't think he had. But then he put the instrument carefully to one side, took my face between his hands and kissed me softly on both cheeks.

"You may not know it, darling," he whispered in my ear "but I have missed you every single day of your life."

How can anyone make you love them so instantly?

I lay my head on his knee and he stroked my hair, never taking his eyes from Connie's. I was all he'd left of value between them. The only remaining link.

I saw her shake her head sadly and put her arm round Giulia. I could only assume either she'd lost her wits or they both loved Giulia very much.

Here was the world's most desirable man pining for her all his adult life, and she clearly adored him.

But Giulia was childlike in her innocence. It would have been like beating a baby. The tragedy was, she knew what she was getting into before it happened. And she chose her own path.

Chapter Twelve
The Click

Christie

"Well," said Gil decidedly. "I'm taking my daughter for a burger."

When everyone jumped up ready to go, he added:

"And none of you – not one of you – is invited."

"Just one cotton-pickin' moment!" I exclaimed. "Don't I get a say in this?"

"No."

My Dad in Champaign had never spoken to me like that. He always considered my feelings.

Gil walked me to the door and, without another word from anyone, we left. He backed Giulia's car out of the carport and set off down the road towards Venice.

"I hate it down here" I said, grumpily.

His behavior had annoyed me. He might be a rock star, but he was my Pa – I liked that, Pa. He might have shaken hands with the Queen of England, but he wasn't talking to me like that. I put my tongue out at him.

Great, Christie, very mature!

He howled with laughter. He'd the most infectious laugh ever - he was entirely captivating. Bastard!

At that precise moment I was struck by an awful thought. What if he didn't like me? I was pretty ordinary, hair apart. No particular skills. I enjoyed a bit of sketching and plinkity-plonking on the piano – pathetic by his standards. I'd better shut my big fat mouth before he left.

"There's the best burger bar in LA down there. I never asked – you do like burgers I take it? Oh shit, you're not vegetarian are you?"

The expression on his face was so appalled it was my turn to laugh.

"Maybe."

"Nope – not possible. You can't have my genes and live on lettuce."

Fortunately, he wasn't wrong. I was as big a carnivore as he could have wanted.

The inside of the restaurant was fitted out like a wild west saloon. There was a Colt rifle displayed above the bar and a dozen bottles of assorted whiskeys on a glass shelf beneath it.

"Howdy folks, what kin I get y'all? Oh, it's you Gil" he reverted to his usual Southern California accent.

"Just passing through, Jake. Just eating today."

"Shucks, man!" said Jake, half Billy the Kid and half himself.

Gil led us through swing doors into a restaurant in the same style as the bar, but with disposable paper table-cloths on the tables.

"Not exactly the Ritz but the food's great" he said, looking round.

"Jeez!" I exclaimed, unable for the moment to think

of anything better.

We ordered a couple of burgers and I watched in bemusement as he carefully peeled every bit of salad off and left it on the side of his plate, then spread it with ketchup and mustard. And he was grief-stricken by his weight problem? Seemed to me everyone was far too lenient with this guy.

He smiled his winning smile and I really saw, firsthand, why everyone gave in to him. That did need to stop.

These were the biggest burgers I ever saw in my life. I only managed half and I'm no slouch. He ate the lot. We finished at the same time. He'd a beer. I drank a diet coke. I was curvy but I knew why. For him there seemed to be no correlation whatever between food and waistline.

He'd ketchup in his beard so I handed him a napkin. That engaging grin again.

"Tell me what you've been doing for the past eighteen years" he said. "I need all the details. There's a lot to catch up on."

A young waitress was doing the rounds lighting small candles on the tables. For a moment Gil appeared mesmerized by the flame and I remembered what Harry had said about his love of candlelight. I drew his attention back to our conversation.

"It's a bit hard to know where to begin. Things didn't start to get weird until I met Giulia in a wood near the University where my father – sorry, Julius - worked. I was about thirteen, I think. All I remember about her

The Twinkle in Pa's Eye

is that she was tiny and wearing a beautiful bracelet like raindrops.

"Yes. I know the one - I bought it for her."

"It struck me she was like one of Cicely Barker's flower fairies. I was only little." I added the last as an excuse and blushed, embarrassed, but he became thoughtful and scratched his beard. I wasn't fond of facial hair but that sixties hippy look did suit him. It gave him a sort of romantic, cavalier appearance.

"Yes, I can see why you would think that. I used to think, when she was a child, she looked as if she could fly. So light and dainty."

"You mustn't be angry with her for having me followed. She'd the best of intentions. She just wanted me to be safe. At first it felt spooky, but I soon got used to it."

"How did you know they all knew each other?"

"Connie gave me this." I pulled the medallion out of my t-shirt for him to see. He was taken aback and didn't look happy.

"I gave that to her before I completely fucked everything up.

"The Movement seemed to be about everything I'd always believed, and I wanted so much to share it with her."

His thoughts did't look to be happy ones. He picked up the medallion and rubbed it between his fingers. Then he looked me deep in the eyes and said:

"It could have been so different for us all. If only I could be what your mother wanted me to be.

The Twinkle in Pa's Eye

"Have any of them talked about me to you? Harry, Connie and the others?"

"Sure. They all love you to bits. What the hell do you have to be sorry for? Unless it's leading us all on a merry dance round LA's less salubrious areas."

He grabbed my hand and, when I tried to pull away, tightened his grip.

I didn't know this guy. Was this a threat? I must have looked alarmed because he dropped my hand back on the table with a muttered 'Sorry'.

"I mess up everything I touch. I'm not good emotionally. Look how I treated your mother and your brothers. How can any human being do that?"

"You could try and untangle the awful mess between you Giulia and Connie. But you can't put the clock back so it can only begin here and now."

"You are a wise soul" he said. "Please help me."

This was no wind-up – he was seriously asking me to help him.

I was eighteen, spoilt, unsophisticated, sometimes stupid. What the hell could I do for this handsome, immensely talented human being who seemed to have a heart of gold and was adored by everyone who knew him. Yet here he was clinging onto my hand and begging me for help.

I pulled back, momentarily bewildered.

"I'll take you back to Connie's" he said and waved the waitress over to pay the bill.

"No. Don't do that yet. We don't know each other and

it's all happening a bit fast for me to take in. I'm asking you to please be patient with me. There is so much to learn about each other. Eighteen years can't be covered over a burger."

"Of course it can't. But I would like us to spend more quality time together, so we can try. If that's okay with you. There are also things I'd like to take you to see."

"If you want, you can meet Simm tomorrow. He's coming up from San Clemente."

Again that fleeting grin.

"What father ever liked his daughter's boyfriend?"

Chapter Thirteen

A Man of Extremes

Christie

I met Simm at Santa Monica pier the following lunchtime, to take him back to Connie's.

He'd never been there before. He'd known Connie's mother had an apartment in Santa Monica but had never had occasion to go.

Apart from me – I liked to think – Connie was the most precious person in the world to him. Even more than Grace which was astonishing. She'd supported him through a very difficult childhood with Oliver, and his sister Deborah. He was too modest to understand Connie had needed him too.

He was leaning against a post of the pier's entrance when I found him. He looked sad and tired. Poor Simm. How could I have been so thoughtless.

I ran into his arms and held him tightly.

"Simm, Simeon, my Simm….." I began.

"If you start apologizing, I'm going home," he laughed.

I could never have told him how sorry I was. I had completely forgotten him for two whole days.

"C'mon. You'll be glad to see Connie again. I know you've met Pa Robson. But I'd like to give you a chance to change your opinion because I think I quite like him. And then there's Harry and Davy and all the rest of them."

"You call him Pa? Does he know? Bit demeaning for a world-famous rock star, wouldn't you say?"

"No, I've thought it but never said it out loud. I know you will love him even though he can be freakin' hard work at times. Excuse my language," I said as an after-thought.

He kissed me enthusiastically.

"Don't stop. I love your eccentricities," he said in an effort to irritate me.

"Come on. They're all waiting. Especially Pa - don't you dare tell him!"

When we got there, with the exception of Connie, they were all lined up like soldiers to greet him. Gil must have arranged it. I determined to call him Pa at the first opportunity.

As was the intention, Simm was completely overwhelmed. Oh boy, would I get Gil for this! The bastard was actually grinning.

Instead of shaking Simm's hand, though, he smiled broadly and hugged him. The air left my lungs in a rush.

He proceeded to introduce everyone.

"This is Harry Forster and David Elliot – you'll have heard of them, vaguely. And this is your Uncle Bobby, Connie's brother – oh, you know him naturally."

"As it happens, I don't," said Simm "But I am glad to

meet you."

"So you're the ones responsible for scaring my gal to death all these years," said my father.

"That's not true," I said. "You know that's not true."

I slapped his arm.

"Simm, you and I are going to get along just fine," said Gil.

"Big of you, Pa." I said pointedly.

The son-of-a-bitch had the nerve to look delighted.

We walked down by the ocean and ate lobster at a waterside restaurant. It was hard to believe that two days ago Pa – great name, I liked it - was half-dead and suicidal – now he was the life and soul of the party.

They had all been right. I had wondered why they were so careful with him. But it seemed to be true almost anything could set him off.

He saw my serious face and winked and smiled. But he knew what I was thinking.

Pa got his lobster and we went through the same procedure as in the burger bar. The fish was pushed to one side and the salad garnish neatly peeled off onto a side-plate. Then the space was filled with fries.

This seemed to be a well-known quirk as all the others were grinning at each other.

"What?" he said when he looked up and noted everyone's expressions.

"Oh, nothing," said Dave.

"I don't like rabbit food. What's wrong with that?"

"Nothing at all," said Giulia, patting his hand.

As we walked back and the guys were using a drinks can as a baseball and lobbing it to each other, Pa took me to one side.

"Do you think Simm could spare you for a couple of hours tomorrow? There's something I'd like to show you, someone I'd like you to meet."

"I don't know but I'll ask him. Is it important?"

"To me, yes."

When I asked, Simm simply said to enjoy myself. He should spend quality time with Connie anyway. He hadn't seen her for a while.

He wanted us to have dinner alone that evening so he could explain what was happening with Grace's estate. It would be good to be alone together after all the upset of the last few days.

I told him that wouldn't be a problem in any case. Pa and Bobby were packing up to go on tour. Giulia had already arranged a shopping expedition with her friend Lucy and was pleased to spend some time in girl-talk. Harry and David just wanted a night on the town. Sorted!

Chapter Fourteen
Beloved Spirit

Christie

I was late up the following morning and found a distressed Pa pacing back and forth in Connie's living room. He'd slept on the sofa and looked like it. Well and truly blitzed. There was only Connie, Gil, Simm and me in the apartment. The rest had disappeared.

He stuck a cup of lukewarm coffee in one of my hands and a cold toasted bagel in the other.

"I made you these," he said abruptly. "Get going."

I had a good swallow of the coffee and a bite of bagel, then he grabbed my hand and pulled me down the stairs.

"Woah!" I said at the bottom. "I don't move that fast for an earthquake this time in a morning. Control yourself!"

He looked shame-faced but was still hopping from foot to foot.

"C'mon," he said impatiently. "You won't move for an earthquake, but I would for where we're going."

He jumped into the driver's seat of Connie's Mustang – he didn't like American cars, they were shit – and keyed it to life. I could only assume Connie had given them to him the night before. Either that, or he'd stolen them from her purse.

Once we were on the way, he calmed down a little but

was still preoccupied and tense. It gave me time to study him closer. Everything before had happened in such a rush I really hadn't done that. Even in the restaurant.

He was in his early forties but looked much older, stockily built with a barrel chest. His hair was collar length, center-parted and extremely glossy. It was clear he was proud of his beard – it was barbered to within an inch of its life but with three days extra growth, which had marred the edges. He'd cloud blue eyes which changed to grey when he was agitated as he was at the moment.

His best feature was his nose, which was the kind of nose women want from plastic surgery and never quite achieve – straight, smallish and narrow. I was very pleased to say I'd inherited it. I could have done without the rest, but the nose was definitely a plus – and Connie's hair, of course.

His voice was low, extremely quiet and had a breathless quality. I'd heard a couple of his records. How the hell did he change it so much to sing?

He drove through central Los Angeles then down miles of bush-lined concrete freeway with frequent overpasses.

At one point we could see to the right what looked like mile after mile of soulless square houses set in grids. Each had a patch of parched grass front and back with the occasional sad-looking tree dotted here and there. It seemed to stretch for miles.

After the best part of an hour of absolute silence he

suddenly said:

"That's where I grew up. Haven't been there in a decade. Don't intend ever going there again."

He relapsed into silence.

Gee, that was a surprise. What mountains he must have had to climb to be where he was now?

Clearly his mind was running along the same lines. His eyes had moistened, and he wiped them on his sleeve impatiently.

A few miles further on we turned off the freeway into a maze of small shop-lined streets, with concrete apartment blocks. He swung with ease down roads so narrow they were only big enough to take passing traffic. I guessed we were nearing the ocean again.

Soon I recognized where we were. Did he have a death wish?

He pulled onto the curb beside the very same cemetery gates we'd dragged him through two days earlier. I grabbed his arm to stop him.

"What are you doing? This is an awful place for you. Why do you want to come here?"

"Be cool" he said. That was the first time I'd heard him speak like a rock star. I hoped it was the last.

He got out of the car, came round and opened my door, helping me out. Then he reached into the back seat and took out a bunch of yellow roses he must have bought before I even stirred that morning. I wondered if he had slept at all.

"Please don't go in there. It can't be good for you."

I grabbed his hand again.

"The opposite, sweetheart. This is where I go when I feel sad - to visit my brother Jamie. Sometimes he speaks to me, sometimes he doesn't. You need to know this weird thing about me, or you won't know me at all."

He was frightened, petrified I wouldn't be able to understand. If I couldn't understand what happened in the next few minutes, we would be doomed to face each other across a bottomless chasm for the rest of time.

He tucked my hand into the crook of his elbow and led me through the gates. It was mid-afternoon and the sun shone through the leaves of the trees, dappling the lawns beneath.

Jamie's grave was no more than twenty yards beyond the gate. I had been too preoccupied to notice much about it last time I was here.

It was quite beautiful, a small lawn surrounded by miniature rose bushes with a carved stone of pale grey marble at one side.

Gil walked straight over the lawn, picked up a metal rose vase and filled it from a tap nearby. Together we arranged the flowers.

His face fell.

"I was carrying flowers like these, in this exact same spot the day after Jamie's funeral – the day your mother and I….."

"Made me?" I asked, helpfully. His mouth quirked.

"Good job," he said, and I could see in some way I had lightened his load.

When he'd finished, he stood back to quietly observe his handiwork. He listened for a moment or two then said:

"Come, Come on."

He kissed my brow and hugged me.

"It was one in a million chance he would come."

"Who?"

But then who should run up the path but Sunny. What the…. what was he doing here? Now the others had backed off it never occurred to me he wouldn't do the same. He flicked his sun-drenched hair out of his eyes, donning shades. He was so out of tune with the peace of this place I was momentarily stunned.

"Hey, babe! How're ya doin?'"

I was gob-smacked. This was only the second time he'd spoken to me. He seemed to go out of his way to avoid talking.

I glanced at Gil. He hadn't moved a muscle. How odd!

"Pa?" I said, "Are you okay?"

"Pa?" said Sunny and doubled up with laughter, the idiot.

"Sure. Just coming." He walked straight past Sunny as if he hadn't seen him.

"You sure you're okay?" I frowned.

Why was he doing this?

"This is my friend Sunny. Please say hello. He's been looking after me like the others."

He frowned in puzzlement then it was as if the sun had come from behind a cloud.

"I don't see him, Christie. Describe him. Describe him now…PLEASE!"

"What? You don't see him? What'd you mean you don't see him? He's standing with his hand on your shoulder."

"Describe him!" he reiterated, raising his voice. Sunny pushed back his hair and chuckled.

"Well, there's no way he's anything other than Californian" I said, feeling like a fool because the more I spoke, the more Sunny laughed. "He looks as if he spends his life on the beach. Deep tan, sun-bleached brown hair. Irritating laugh."

I glowered at Sunny, and he convulsed again.

"Stop Gil. This is no way to impress your recently discovered daughter."

"Believe me Christie, you are seeing someone I wish with all my soul I could see. But I can't. That's my brother Jamie."

"Sure is!" said Sunny, giving me a thumbs up. Of a sudden his face became sad.

"I love you, Christie. Please tell Gil we'll both wait for him, and you'll see me only a couple more times."

Then – poof! – he was gone. My mouth fell open and I spun on my heel to look at my Pa. Momentarily, I was lost for words, then I said:

"He left a message for you, I'll repeat it verbatim. I've no idea what it means.

"He said 'I love you Christie. Please tell Gil we'll both wait for him and you'll - me presumably – see me only a couple more times."

Pa wept. I let him and when he was in control again, he said:

"The first was typical Jamie. Instead of hugging someone or even shaking hands, he would tell them he loved them. But, clearly, you he does love or he wouldn't have stuck around and let you see him.

"The second is to tell me he and…someone else– no idea who, bit worrying – will wait for me when I pass. He's implying it won't be too long."

Perhaps that was relative. I hoped so.

He looked me deep in the eyes and held my gaze for some seconds.

"I can't tell you what a relief that will be. My whole life has been such a struggle and I am just so tired. Your coming has lifted a burden. The others kept an eye on you, but Jamie took care of you, body and soul."

I choked on a sob.

"Oh Pa, please don't say that. Your life may have been made difficult by some, but there are far more who love you and always will. Otherwise, they'd have given up on you long ago. And what about your audiences? Wouldn't you miss them and the joy you give them, the love they give back?"

He brightened immediately.

"Will you come to one of our gigs? Then you can see for yourself what I mean. I'd like you to stand where you can see what I see, then you'll know what I mean. Jamie always felt it, too."

I cuddled up to him:

"Come on. He won't be here anymore so you don't need to visit unless you want to. Let's go home."

"Giulia and I will stay with Connie until I leave. I know – very weird. I take it you and Simm will be going back to San Clemente. Could I visit when I come back?"

"Wherever I am, you will be welcome," I replied.

Chapter Fifteen

Grace's Revenge

Christie

The following day Simm and I took the Ocean Walk towards Venice. I could only assume it had changed a lot from the days of sun and surf when 'dudes' like Jamie walked the sands, and 'honeys' in bikinis with transistors giggled on the beach.

Now it was rather sad. Couples with pushchairs sucking on ice cream cones strolled past kaftan-strewn stalls. Teenagers with dreadlocks swung from dilapidated fitness rings on the concrete beach-side. Food wrappers blew along the paving slabs in the ocean breeze. Pa's burger joint was a jewel by comparison.

We walked on until we began to feel the effects of the sun, then turned and walked back again.

We'd decided to drive along the coast, have an early dinner and drive back to San Clemente that evening. We'd imposed on Connie for too long as it was.

Grace's paperwork was best examined at home in any case. There would be more privacy, more leisure. It would probably take up to a year for the Probate Office in Chicago to okay and publish the Will, but Simm had a copy for us to look at.

Then I really had to go back to Champaign to see my parents. Poor things must have thought I'd emigrated.

I hugged my Pa before I left and told him the trial period was over as far as I was concerned, and he was a hit. He said he was relieved to hear that, as he'd known his decision the moment he clapped eyes on me. I smiled to myself, knowing that wasn't true.

He'd be in touch he said about the gig, and would I please bring Simm with me? He shook Simm warmly by the hand and told him to take care of his little girl for him. Simm pulled him into a man-hug I could see pleased Pa hugely. He'd be a good father-in-law.

What? Now where had that thought come from? It seemed I was always a country mile ahead of Simm when it came to our relationship!

We drove down to San Clemente in glorious sunshine – not too warm – which drew glitter from the azure ocean and lace edging from the waves which lapped ashore.

That I had finally found Pa and that he was a father who, although unknow to me except by reputation for almost the whole of my life, I had learned very personal things about, things I suspected he'd never shared with another living soul.

I glanced across at Simm, absorbed by his own thoughts and the drive. He was so wonderful.

His tanned face was smooth, and when he glanced my way his eyes sparkled brighter than the ocean with love. My life could have been so different. Yet for the whole of it I had been cared for, often by total strangers, and of course a ghost. How many people could claim that?

Simm looked my way quizzically.

"Oh nothing," I said. "Just happy, I guess."

He reached across and squeezed my hand, holding it in his lap.

That ocean drive was such a pleasurable experience that the journey flashed by and soon we were pulling up the hill to Grace's retreat, lined with her beloved rhododendrons.

Every inch of this place was filled with memories, especially for Simm. I hugged him close to me as we walked forward. An occasional tick in his jaw was all that gave away his inner turmoil.

At the door, he turned towards me and kissed me for comfort and strength. He rested his head on my shoulder for a few seconds before turning his key in the lock.

The interior was cool and dark after the bright sunshine. And absolutely silent. Simm had sent the staff off while he was away and they wouldn't return until the following day. I was glad they weren't there.

He hadn't been out on Grace's favorite place, the terrace overlooking the town and the ocean beyond. He said without me he just couldn't face it.

"Once we've settled in, we are going to walk every inch of Ginsling House until you are used to it and have chased all your blues away. Grace wouldn't have wanted it any other way."

He smiled a tight smile:

"I can just imagine what she'd say. 'Idiot boy. Quit your moaning this minute. You're a Maxwell. Don't ever forget it'."

It was so Grace, we both laughed.

I glanced through the glass wall which led out onto the terrace. The furniture was still covered in protective wraps.

"You go and fix us some coffee and I'll sort out the terrace."

I sat on one of the sofas alone for a few minutes, deep in thought of times past, and soon he arrived with the coffee.

"It might be easier on here," he said, placing the tray on the tiled table. "The papers are quite large."

There was a fat parchment envelope balanced on the edge of the tray.

"You haven't opened it. Why not?"

"I just couldn't. I needed you here."

He ran his hand through his hair and murmured:

"I'm such a coward, Christie. What do you see in me?"

"I'm not even going to dignify that with an answer. Come on, let's do it."

He spread the documents out on the table and smoothed them with his palm. There were three sheets of parchment with the usual preamble of the 'sound mind' bit on page one.

Sheet two got down to the nitty-gritty. The bequests. I knew this had nothing to do with personal gain for Simm. It was just a thing he'd to get through as quickly as possible.

Grace wouldn't have passed up the chance to let everyone know what she thought of them, so I was looking forward to this enormously, even if he wasn't.

To her 'adored grandson', Simeon Maxwell, she'd left fifty million dollars. Well, that might have surprised Simm but I couldn't imagine why. I could see, even through his tan, he'd gone white. He sat down suddenly. I handed him his coffee.

"Come on," I said to distract him. "What's next?"

"She's also left me her Rolls," he continued, faintly.

"I wouldn't read too much into that – she hated the thing." I said to lighten his mood.

"I leave one thousand dollars to my son Oliver Maxwell for the love he bore his father...."

Despite his depression, Simm almost choked.

"...on the proviso he share it with his daughter Deborah."

"I'll tell you later," he said.

The house and its contents in Windham she'd left to Connie on condition she didn't sell it within ten years. It was packed with original paintings and antique furniture and china, which in themselves, were priceless.

There was absolutely no chance at all that Oliver was not going to contest this Will.

"The residue of my estate I leave to my much-loved adopted granddaughter, Anna Christina Robson Maxwell aka Anna Christina Heywood, to be detailed upon proving of this my last Will and Testament."

Having his name linked with mine I knew would delight Pa.

Knowing Grace, 'the residue' would probably also be a hundred bucks.

I knew her thinking. She liked the idea of Simm and I together and even from beyond the grave, was trying to pull a few strings.

This last surprised Simm, though. It was so ambiguous and so unlike straight-talking Grace, he couldn't figure it out.

The last entry which affected me directly was for my foster parents:

"To Julius and Catherine Heywood, presently of Champaign in the State of Illinois, one thousand dollars to be paid annually in perpetuity. This last in gratitude for the love and protection shown to my adopted granddaughter, Anna Christina."

The rest of the Will was bequests of various small amounts of money to employees – she didn't appear to have any relations – at least none she spoke to.

Simm sat back in his chair, still in a state of shock.

"I need something stronger than coffee."

He got up and fixed himself a stiff whisky which he'd

drunk half of before he got back to the table.

"I'm a multi-millionaire," he said faintly.

"Well, you are at the moment, but your Dad hasn't got his hands on the Will just yet. You do realize he will contest it, don't you?"

Simm turned the Will to the last page which was two-thirds filled with terms attached to the bequests.

One of the items was a clause which read

"Should any legatee contest this Will for any reason whatsoever, they will have their bequest withdrawn."

"Guess she covered everything. I wish I could be a fly on the wall when your Dad finds out."

"I'll tell you about Grandpa Alec's death if you wish," said Simm.

I was doubtful. I got the impression even Connie didn't know, and feared he was showing too much trust in me, too soon.

"I don't think you should tell me. Grace may have considered it breaking a confidence."

"She thought of you as her granddaughter, her family."

He proceeded to relate a story even Edgar Alan Poe couldn't have concocted.

"Grace's husband, my Grandpa Alec, died in an accident. He liked to go shooting, mostly wild turkey. Anyway, when Dad was in his late teens, eighteen I

The Twinkle in Pa's Eye

think, Grandpa, took him out with him for the day. Dad had been a competitive marksman in his school days and loved the sport.

"They enjoyed a really good day together and when they returned home, Alec insisted Dad follow procedure and clean his gun before putting it away in the cabinet. Dad said he'd other, more pressing jobs and he'd sort it out later.

An argument broke out during which Alec was punched and fell, cracking his head on the corner of the gun cabinet.

I don't exactly know where Dad went, but Gran found her husband lying in a pool of blood sometime later. He'd bled to death. That's the story which has come down through the family. True? I don't know for sure.

"Rather than cut him off altogether," Simm continued, "she gave him sufficient money to set up in business and told him if ever he came back, she'd go to the police. She even relented on that eventually. Once Deborah and I came along she felt she'd no other choice.

"She loved Connie on sight and couldn't understand what she saw in my Dad. She was proved right.

"Connie knew nothing of Alec's death, of course. But she did know he'd a nasty temper.

"When Connie and Gil were going through their separation, he behaved appallingly to him."

I leaned over the terrace rail gazing down at the crowds, made silent by distance below, and tried to picture Pa and Connie before their lives became so sad.

Chapter Sixteen

The Love of Three Men

Christie

Pa did come to stay a little over a week later. He looked a complete wreck once more. We sorted out a suite of rooms for him near the back of the house where it was cool. That way he could have time to himself if he wanted.

I was amazed to see a real friendship had developed between Pa and my boyfriend. But then he was such a sweetheart – kind and patient – it was difficult not to love him, as Connie had said.

And Simm? Apart from when he lost Grace, always upbeat and with a ready smile.

Neither had had an easy time with people they loved or even liked. Simm'd had Connie to cling to, but I got the impression Pa had only had the very flawed Jamie, and he so desperately missed him.

Pa only shared meals with us for the first couple of days. I got the impression he slept for much of the time. On the third day he arrived at the breakfast table, freshly showered and stylishly clothed, looking happier and more relaxed than I had seen him.

"Thank you both - I needed time to sort myself out. Running on all cylinders now.

"If you don't mind, I'll stay another couple of days

then head back to LA. We've a few new sidemen to bring up to speed for the next tour. I really am getting too old for this. Only a week off then straight back to work. I shouldn't have allowed myself to get sucked back in once I'd left – even if it is only for live shows."

For a moment the weariness reappeared in his eyes, but he quickly shook it off. A lifetime of mistreatment had had that effect on him. He'd learned to lock everything away.

"It's hardly surprising you can't do now what was a breeze as a teen. You should give yourself a break," said Simm.

"I'm not sure they'd cope. My friends make up a large proportion of their audiences.

"Isn't it just amazing these wonderful people turn up to hear me sing after all these years? So many faces I see over and over. I could never thank them enough. Now they are accompanied by children and grandchildren. It's such a privilege to sing for them."

He drew one of my hands to his mouth and kissed it, then laid it against his cheek. I could see Simm was getting emotional as well, so I braced my shoulders:

"Well, one of us has to take control of this situation," I said shakily.

"I love you Christie," said Simm, inadvertently starting the waterworks again, goddam. My father merely smiled but his expression said the same.

Pa returned to LA and two days later a letter arrived

with a couple of back-stage passes for a show in Chicago a week later.

I'd called Mom and Dad to say I'd be back to stay for a while and would be bringing my boyfriend with me.

It was a shame the Windham house had been mothballed pending the outcome of Probate, but for Pa's gig we could drive to Chicago – it was only two or three hours – stay overnight and travel back to Champaign the following day.

My Mom and Dad were delighted to see us. I could tell they were put out that I'd not kept them up to date with what was happening, but they were infinitely polite and managed to swallow their annoyance in front of Simm. Afterall this was only a boyfriend. Eighteen-year-old girls had lots of them.

My father gave one of his rare smiles and firmly shook Simm's hand. My effusive mother pulled him into a hug and kissed his cheek. Simm, of course, was perfect. He always was.

I wondered in passing how they'd have got along with Pa. I suppose he'd have exchanged a few confidences, smiled that wicked smile and they'd have been as captivated as the rest of the world. He hid his sadness so well.

When my mother mortified me by putting us in separate rooms, Simm merely smiled his thanks. She didn't get the same response from me - I scowled at her.

It only took a few hours until I crept into his room in the dead of night. We made passionate but silent love and I crept back again in the first light of dawn. It was actually fun - made me feel naughty.

The following morning, we took a stroll round Champaign and around the University campus so he could see where I'd grown up.

I showed him where I'd run into Harry and how he had comforted me when I was so upset with my Illinois parents for taking me to Austin to hide me from Pa. I told him about running into people with medallions who seemed to be chasing me here there and everywhere over the continental US of A, and all the other disasters, major and minor, which had made up my life to date.

After I'd finished my tale of woe and he was beginning to look sorry for me, I told him how I'd grown to love the people I thought of as my guardians and depend upon them for my safety, even if they had had me tearing my hair out on occasion. Of course, I'd then to tell him about my run-in with Ed – the only time they'd ever let me down.

After, we walked to the Arboretum where I had spent so many happy hours putting pencil to paper when I was younger. I told him of my first meeting with Giulia and the conversation of strangers, how kind I thought she was, and about the beautiful dewdrop bracelet she wore.

That seemed to jog something in his mind. He reached into his pocket and pulled out a small silk-covered box and opened it. Sinking to his knees in front of the log seat we were sharing, and regardless of the leaf-mold, he uttered the immortal words:

"I love you more than my own life, Christie. Please be my wife."

I wish I could say my acceptance was graceful but, let's face it, this was me and it was never going to be anything of the kind.

"Oh for chrissake, Simm, we've only been together a matter of weeks. How can you ask a question like that?"

"We've always had Connie in common," he said, visibly upset.

"That's nothing to do with you and me!"

The fact of the matter was I was dying to say yes but was scared to death.

Then I actually looked at the contents of the box and I probably would have married him for the ring.

It was seven shaped baguette diamonds fashioned like an olive spray which curved slightly towards the tip. It glittered and sparkled pure white in the afternoon sun. It was absolutely the most beautiful piece of jewelry I had ever seen and that included Giulia's bracelet. When I finally recovered the faculty of speech I said:

"Well…an engagement could be a long one. That'd give us time. You can always have it back if things don't work out."

He grinned. Clearly he'd read my mind. I nudged him

with a fake scowl.

"I take it that's a 'yes'," he whispered, kissing me softly on the lips. "I think perhaps it might be wise not to give your mother the vapors and let her know before you wear it."

He'd already got her number.

"And my Dad," I added. "He doesn't say much but he's just as emotional. If it's okay with you I'd also like to speak to Pa but as you two are now best buddies, I can't imagine he'll have any objections.

"Perhaps it won't fit," I said optimistically.

He was openly laughing at me by this point.

"Sure. You absolutely have to try it on – just to be on the safe side."

Oh God, I loved him – and his taste in engagement rings.

Mom was shelling peas in the kitchen when we got back to the house. Everyone else in the world ate frozen ones, but not my mother.

I jumped up onto the counter and grabbed a handful – so much better uncooked. She slapped my hand away as she had when I was little.

"Not a good way to start discussing our announcement, wouldn't you say?" said Simm, amused.

My mother's head snapped up and she eyed us both suspiciously.

"Sorry, Mrs. Heywood," said my beloved, "We'll

need to speak to both you and your husband together. When will he be home?"

At that very moment the door slammed, my Dad put his head round the door and asked what time dinner would be.

"Oh, not any time soon, I'd imagine," I said innocently..

Simm grabbed me by the arm and marched me from the house and down the road.

"Give your Dad time to get in the house before you drop a bombshell on him."

"If you knew the number of bombs he's dropped on me in the past year, you might be less sympathetic," I complained.

Nonetheless, we walked increasingly quickly round several blocks and ran back through the front door.

Mom and Dad were initially dubious. They said I was too young and inexperienced. I should play the field more.

Simm was better than I was at this. He showed them the ring and watched their mouths drop open.

They asked lots of questions I didn't have a clue about but which Simm had obviously spent some time thinking out.

"Have you an idea of when the wedding will be?"

I knew this was to ascertain that there actually was a wedding in the offing, and this wasn't just a ploy on my part to wear the coolest ring in Christendom.

"Perhaps in the Spring?" he lifted an eyebrow in my direction.

My thoughts instantly filled with orange-blossom coronets and running through flower-laden meadows in a flowing dress. He was there, naturally, in a tuxedo which would have looked pretty weird in a meadow.

I cuddled up to him and gazed into his eyes.

My father still looked dubious, but slightly less so.

"I would like an undertaking from you both there will be no children until Christie is at least twenty-one," he said.

Which I guess was a pretty standard request for an underage daughter.

Chapter Seventeen
Shocked and Bewildered

Christie

We had a joyous few days together, Simm and I, before heading off to Chicago to see Pa. I was curious to see how he'd work. I had a feeling he was something of a control freak which was probably part of his problem.

Simm drove. That way I could wiggle my finger around to admire the sunlight striking sparks from my ring. Every time he caught me doing it his face lit up, but as we neared the city, I put it back in its box. One thing at a time.

The concert venue was in an eighty-year-old building which had had its innards ripped out and recreated for modern performances.

On production of the passes, we were shown into the Green Room back-stage where a waiter fetched us drinks. There were a few other people there I took to be wives or girlfriends. And a couple of guys smoking something suspicious in a corner.

It was quite interesting watching people dashing back and forth from the wings to the changing rooms along the corridor outside.

I glimpsed Pa hurry by once. He seemed to be holding three conversations at once and his head was turning this way and that. He was half-dressed with his shirt hanging out and his belt loose. Apart from when I'd seen him propping up a gravestone, this is the only time I'd seen him look disheveled.

I checked my watch. He was due on stage in ten minutes. He looked as if he'd at least twenty minutes of getting ready to do. But within five he hurried into the Green Room, hugged and kissed me and grinned broadly at Simm.

As I wiped his stage make-up off my cheek he said:

"Good timing. I've to go now but I'll get Bobby to show you were to stand."

"Bobby's playing with you? Oh great. It'll be good to see him."

He ran for the door faster I was sure, than was good for a middle-aged man, and disappeared towards the stage. Within seconds, Bobby appeared and took us to a place in the wings where we had a clear view without being seen. Then he, too, disappeared.

To the side and slightly forward from our position was a microphone. Gil's guitars, four of them, were being stood on racks to the side of a building block of amps. Technicians were running, crouching, around the darkened stage making last minute adjustments.

Sidemen picked up or sat quietly at their instruments and waited. Then suddenly there was blackness and complete silence. The audience stilled.

A spotlight on center stage lit a solitary figure.

"And, here, especially for you…. the world's number one band…'California Crystal'," he thundered. The applause was deafening.

The backing band struck up as the singers ran on stage. Pa managed to sidle up and plant a kiss on my cheek on the way past. I brushed his stage makeup off my black lace top. At this rate there'd be more on me than him.

He fastened his guitar strap over his shoulder and gave me a wink. And from then on I got the impression an earthquake wouldn't have gained his attention.

He opened his mouth to sing, and I swore the world stood still. Perfect notes soared into the auditorium, some so high and soft they seemed to melt. I looked at Simm – he appeared as bewildered as I felt. The hairs had stood up on the back of my neck. We were standing practically next to him, so it was much different from the auditorium at Anaheim.

From our vantage point, we could see most of the audience. He was singing a slow ballad and a sea of upturned faces spread before him, each looking as I felt.

I truly had had no idea what he'd meant when he called them his 'friends' but I knew now and that was after just one song.

The next was a raunchy, rock number requiring a different sound, so he only sang backing but he spent the entire number covertly conducting the backing band and giving them their cues.

The crowd began to dance. The energy they radiated was phenomenal. I looked at Pa's face. His expression was euphoric. The other guys too.

By the middle of the show, it was apparent that

audience and band were one entity, feeding off each other, lifting each other higher and higher.

Then came *the* song. The one he sang as a gift to his friends in the audience. Every show they demanded it and no matter what, that song was always sung for them. He was a serious performer but, when he sang this song, he turned and smiled into their faces as if they were *personal* friends, which I supposed they were. There was a momentary pause then rapturous applause.

Up close as we were, we could see tears of sheer emotion making runnels through what remained of his stage makeup. Momentarily, he turned away to compose himself then loudly and clearly he thanked the audience for coming to see them.

He could never, never have given this up. It was a drug which had entirely consumed him.

They finished with a medley of old hits going back years. By the time they'd finished I could see he was completely spent. He was soaked in perspiration, his hair plastered to his face. Someone handed him a towel. His chest was heaving as he fought for breath.

My Pa looked absolutely wiped out, but his face was aglow with happiness. He carefully placed his guitar on a stand, strode across the stage and enfolded me in his arms, lifting me clean off my feet.

"Now do you understand?" he panted in my ear. I pressed my cheek to his mutely and borrowed his towel.

He kissed the medallion at his throat. I never knew so much love could emanate from one person - it was almost unbearable, like looking into the sun. Then suddenly he was downcast.

"We can never get them back, all those wasted years."

"C'mon Pa. Shouldn't you shower or something?" I said bracingly.

This world-famous rock icon with probably the best voice in the modern musical world, actually turned and screwed up his face at me like a naughty five-year-old. I thought Simm was going to explode.

"Go have another drink back-stage and I'll shower – thoroughly – and meet you there in an hour or so."

I was happy with that. Plenty of time to indulge my curiosity.

We drank coffee brought to us by a sixteen-year-old so cool he called me 'man' and spat his gum into a bin without breaking step.

Bobby arrived a few minutes after Pa had left. I could hear the ping and clatter of instruments being dismantled and packed away.

"Can I have a look at that electric piano, Bobby? Before they pack it away?" 'and before anyone arrives to stop me having a go' – but I didn't say the last bit.

"The Wurlitzer is mine anyway, so you won't be stepping on anyone's toes."

The three of us returned to the mostly deserted stage

The Twinkle in Pa's Eye

– just one or two technicians were finishing up. Bobby nodded to one of them and said he'd be ready in a few minutes. Ha! No chance, I thought.

Simm had never heard me play before. It was entirely possible he may be rethinking his proposal shortly.

I played a chord and nearly blasted out my eardrums. The instrument was still set up for performance and I was only used to an ordinary acoustic piano. Bobby adjusted the volume and grinned.

"That should be better," he said. I tried again. Yes, infinitely better.

So what to play? I hadn't the first idea - my mind was a complete blank.

"How about 'Georgia on My Mind'?" suggested Bobby who understood my taste.

I am an absolutely awful vocalist - my voice would make a mule sound tuneful – so Bobby sang. No Gil - definitely a rock n roll guy – but pretty good, nonetheless.

We played the song through to the end. I didn't like it. I thought I got more soul from a 'proper' piano, so I moved across to a scratched and battered baby-grand at the side of the stage, which clearly belonged to the venue. It reminded me of the good old days with Dee-Dee and the band.

"Will it be okay?" I asked Bobby.

"Sure. Why not?" he replied.

I pulled out the stool, adjusted it and committing the position of the pedals to memory, opened the lid and trailed my fingertips along the keys. It was without the mellow tone of the battered old wreck at the University but it would do.

I played one or two totally irrelevant chords to get my fingers working again and launched into Chicago Breakdown, Maceo's brilliant piano piece. It was impossibly difficult, but I was so enjoying myself I was hardly aware of the fudged bits.

I was interrupted by Simm banging his palm down on the piano top and digging me in the ribs.

"What?" I said pushing him away, annoyed by the interruption. Then I noticed the auditorium had become unnaturally quiet and looked up.

Pa was standing in the doorway. He'd clearly been in the process of dressing after his shower as he'd one sock on, the other held in his right hand and both shoes in his left. His shirt was unbuttoned.

The expression on his face was scary. He was either so furious he couldn't speak or shocked rigid. I prayed for the second.

He dropped the shoes and strode purposefully over to the piano. Shit, he looked mad!

He hammered his fist on the piano and said abruptly:

"Again. Play it again. Don't argue – just play."

His expression still looked grim.

I slammed down the piano lid.

"No….. I won't," I replied, jumping to my feet and staring, equally belligerent.

By this point we were standing virtually nose to nose, the static between us almost palpable. I saw him take several deep breaths to steady himself as he read my mind…. again.

"Good not bad," he managed with difficulty. His expression had become professional.

I looked at Simm for reassurance - he squeezed my hand. The people in the doorway were looking at each other curiously.

I sat again and put my fingers on the keys.

The boogie-woogie intro was one I was used to, so beginning was easy. It was the rest of it that was difficult. I made a couple of false starts until Gil said:

"You're uptight. Relax."

Easier said than done but I finally settled down and disappeared into the music as I usually did.

It seemed I had no sooner started than I finished. It was always like that, time just slipped away when I played. When I came to the end I whispered "Sorry" and softly closed the lid.

When I finally dared to meet his eye, I found him staring at me as if he couldn't quite believe what I'd done. Good or bad?

"Where did you learn to play like that?" he demanded.

Still no expression to say which way he was going to jump.

"A combination of Bobby and... well, nothing else really. Grace Maxwell had a piano and I played it when I visited. Then she told my Dad to get one and he did."

In the half-dark I'd missed his tears. He lifted me bodily into the biggest hug imaginable.

"I knew it... I knew one of my kids would inherit the gene. It's you. Oh, thank you."

I pushed him away and looked him in the eye just to check he was serious. He seemed to be.

"Can you play any other style?"

"Bobby taught me to play blues, but you'll have to sing if you want lyrics - I sound like a bullfrog."

That finally broke the ice and we were laughing together. I looked at Simm for reassurance. He was grinning from ear to ear. Bobby gave me the A-OK in the background.

"How about 'The Very Thought of You' – I love Billie Holliday's version." Pa agreed with enthusiasm.

It was such a breeze accompanying a voice like his. I felt my fingers fly over the keys, almost of their own volition, the twinkling notes blending and complimenting his effortless vocals.

We were both weeping openly by the end, and I vaguely noticed the small crowd had reassembled at the door. Bobby was jumping up and down and Simm was beside him, shocked rigid.

Gil took my hand and kissed it. I looked at him expectantly.

"Oh no! You're never doing that professionally. You're too good and they'll eat you alive."

"Who will?" What the hell was he talking about?

"The whole musical establishment except me - your own family may disappoint you as well - mine did anyway," he said, contemplating well-manicured nails, sadly.

"But…today is a day for celebration."

"Oh no," I said. "No bars."

"No bars." he agreed and grinned. "How's pizza in Wicker Park sound?"

Chapter Eighteen
Contentment

Christie

They had another gig at the same venue the following evening, so we decided to stop over.

Or rather Simm did. He was really star-struck – even by Bobby, which was a joke. I hoped fervently he'd come down enough to talk to Pa as a human being again. Currently, I could see him strewing his path with palms.

We stood in the same place. The set list had altered quite a bit with the exception of Pa's song, which drew the same rapturous applause. I could see how a jealous individual like Ed would hate it. For all his arrogant flamboyance, he'd nothing to touch the heart like this deceptively simple song of Pa's.

After five or six numbers, someone grabbed me by the hand and before I knew what was happening, dragged me behind the stage to the wings at the other side. Bobby set me down at the piano. I was livid – especially as I knew Gil's fury would probably be aimed at me.

My erstwhile teacher stood back, grinning, with his arms folded. There began to be a hole in the orchestration. Swearing like a sailor I launched into the accompaniment of a song I only had a very basic knowledge of, doing my best to improvise. I'd kill the bastard. But it would have to be later as at present all

The Twinkle in Pa's Eye

I could do was concentrate.

I saw Pa turn round, his expression blank and professional. He motioned to my tormentor to get back to work, and Bobby sidled me off the stool and took over seamlessly. He grinned at Pa who shook his head at him.

> But it had only been teasing on Bobby's part and Pa, after glaring, ignored him completely and the rest of the performance was faultless.

Pa left for pastures new with plenty to think about until we saw each other again. He had been so overwhelmed by what we'd both learned, I think he could have done with a long holiday. But as usual work intervened.

I was ecstatic. My Pa was more than I ever could have imagined – kind, gifted and generous beyond measure.

Every note we'd played together had been magical and I believe for the first time in his entire life, Gil Robson was truly happy.

Also available from Amazon in Kindle, paperback and hard-cover

'The Ultimate Link' series

The off-stage fall and rise of an international rock icon. It's not all fun being world-famous!

Book One - **'Catch a Falling Star'**
Book Two - **'The Twinkle in Pa's Eye'**
Book Three **'The Mountain Monk and Shadow Rider'**

'The Life and Times of Grace Harper Maxwell'

The back-story to the most mysterious and enigmatic character of 'the Ultimate Link' series.

'Bridie O'Neill and Cathal's Ghost'

The story of an Irish New Yorker born into abject poverty who through trials and tribulations lifts herself to a life of luxury in California via Ireland.

The 'Through the Veil' Series

The dubious adventures of an ancient line of Witches from the lonely hills of the English Lake District, and a mischievous neolithic stone circle, the Seven Sisters.

Book One **Witch Stones**
Book Two **Witch Veil**
Book Three **Witch Ethereal**